MAD HATTER

Georgia Helm

A KISMET Romance

METEOR PUBLISHING CORPORATION
Bensalem, Pennsylvania

To Mom and Dad, for steadfast love and support.

To Susan and Gerry, for nudging, nudging!

Special thanks to Tom Hirt, a superior custom hatter and handsome, modest guy.

GEORGIA HELM

Born and raised in the West, Georgia Helm dwells in Arizona among secretly-breeding floppy disks, books, and her empty saddle. She has an affinity for horses, Maine, and people who might have been. Raised on the West's tales, food, music, books, and values, she confesses to a persistent, covetous admiration of Western men, the elusive, handsome few who have earned their big hats and dusty boots. Hope springs eternal. . . .

PROLOGUE

The old-timers—those who'd lie in the Payson, Arizona, Pioneer Cemetery—got good conversational mileage out of how much Owen Dixon resembled old Benjamin. Tall and lean, the same pitchy-black hair, granite-gray eyes, straight nose, angled jaw, and the same crooked, devilish grin. The same fussy nature—not by way of criticism, mind, but in praise of his work. Not many hatters left in the country—maybe in the world, who knew?—made hats by hand, start to finish, with care and pride. Lots of nasty things could get said about Owen's personal life. Oh, he'd settled down some since the old man had died—that'd probably shoved a home truth about life in his face. You could still say Owen had a flip and ornery tongue and a watchful eye for the women—they didn't call him Devil for nothing! Still, when it came to his hats, Benjamin Dixon would have been right proud. Right proud.

The Dixon Hat Company's entrance was narrow and dark, like a tunnel gone askew, flanked by old pine logs, Benjamin's posters, and a big old sign:

SMOKING
IN THIS SHOP
WILL RESULT IN A **BEATING**
PERSONALLY ADMINISTERED
BY THE OWNER

The tunnel was a bottleneck, but unusual, and everybody knew Dixons were unusual. Hardly ever enough same-time customers to clog up a bottleneck, anyway.

Owen's brother, Haddon, used to say it was a security risk. Owen said nobody would bother robbing him for the contents of his old cash register. If they did, he'd change their minds with the .45 under the counter. If it came to a fire, he'd as soon die with his hats as anywhere, so what difference did it make?

The shop had tiny windows—Benjamin believed glass let the winter come straight into his bones. In the old days, hats had been displayed by lamplight, but even Benjamin had been forward thinking enough to install electricity in 1948. Owen was still conservative, not to say stingy. The workbenches had light on a cloudy day, but in the shop area, the old brass fixtures had mighty small bulbs. Hats threw shadows on the floor and across the mirrors. It made a snug kind of place where men could hole up and gab on a rain-drenched day.

ONE

The harness brasses behind the door jangled when Sara Dugan came in.

She dawdled in the tunnel, brushing rain off her jacket, slapping her rain hat against the wall, reading the no-smoking sign Owen's grandfather had painted before she was born. Had anyone ever challenged it? Hard to imagine taciturn old Benjamin engaging in violence. Owen probably hovered in hope that someone would come in and light up.

The warm, peculiar smell of steamed fur, chemicals, and cedar stroked her face familiarly as she inched along the tunnel. What next? Stroll in as if she'd seen Owen yesterday? Then what? Say *Hi*, shake hands? Say *Hi*, throw her arms around him for a big hug? Say *I missed you so much my heart ached every one of the last 1,458 days? Why didn't you call me? Where were you?* . . . Kiss him until he fainted?

Fainted. Right. An outstanding kiss would not be necessary. The mere shock of a kiss from Sara would make him faint. Sara had loved him for years. He didn't know it, or knew but didn't care and, she thought with depressing pragmatism, probably never would.

She was uncomfortable inside her blue sweater. If it hadn't been raining and a few days after Thanksgiving, she might have worn something light and feminine. Her sweater and wool skirt with comfortable flats were appropriate for the circumstance, but she wished she'd chosen something more streamlined. Her fine honey-colored hair was pulled into a knot at her nape as defense against the weather. She wished she'd paid more attention to what the clerk had shown her when she'd invested in new makeup before she'd left Phoenix. She wished she'd lost ten pounds. She wished she were taller. Owen liked sleek, tall women.

Owen was at the workbench behind the counter, his back to her, bent to a partially shaped black hat that quietly pirouetted on a small wheel. One of his large, well-shaped hands applied what resembled a piece of sandpaper to the felt. He didn't turn when she walked in, although she knew he had heard the brasses. He might even know it was she. He'd always had an astonishingly good sense about that. It might have been her own faulty perception, but everything about Owen had always been astonishingly good. Bad, but good. She took a steadying breath and walked toward Owen.

Little had changed since the days when she had dropped in after school, pretending to watch Benjamin do his work but shyly hoping a young, rakish Owen would be there. Felt cowboy hats still clung to the knobs and corners of antique dressers, tables, and mirrors, as they always had. The styles might be slightly different; styles evolved in cowboy hats as in other clothing. Owen made what he liked, and what he liked had the look of time—big dipped or rolled brims and high crowns, simply shaped, that could be mashed by a bronc's hoof and easily reformed by a man's fingers. The hatbands were distinct—leather, horsehair, and silver. Owen made those himself. As well as Sara knew him, the artistic bent in him sometimes amazed her.

The Duke Hat was still on display by the register, protected by its glass box. John Wayne had worn the hat, made for him by Owen's grandfather, in an early movie. The sweatband was supposed to bear the Duke's autograph, but Sara had never seen it. The Duke Hat never left its case.

The potbelly stove, with its coffeepot, companion straight chair, and full woodbox, hadn't changed. The NCR cash register hadn't an electrical part to its name. Its little glass window perpetually announced NO SALE.

The potbelly glowed. Her jacket was already hot. She felt humid and nervous. When would Owen acknowledge her presence? She draped the damp jacket over the chair back and put her manila envelope on the seat.

Owen still didn't turn. He had a supple, naturally athletic, eye-catching body. A black-and-white-checked flannel shirt lay close across his leanly muscled back as he bent—a superior back that Sara had seen naked and browned in the hot summer sun. His hips were trim below a black leather belt with DEVIL tooled across the back. The shadow from one of his own hats, a wide-brimmed gray with a striking black-and-white horsehair band, made it difficult to admire the hair she already knew was straight and stubborn. His hands, manipulating textured paper against the hat, were deft and adorned with little scars.

She had felt those hands on her body. Her heart kicked hard at the memory of a Halloween, with spooky music and the groans of the school's Haunted House in the background. She'd been eighteen, Owen twenty-six. Those scarred hands had thrust her into a dark corner and been the first hands ever to touch her breasts or stroke her hips. Owen's mouth had been the first ever to touch Sara's. He was drunk, she'd thought as she squirmed in his iron grip, writhing under his feverish kisses and astonishingly blatant words, desperately wondering why he was at a childish school party and how she would escape before *something else* happened. The *something else* had been rather vague in her naive, inexperienced mind. Only later had she realized what might have happened if Haddon hadn't come hunting Owen and rescued her. She had truly hated Owen Dixon for a couple of days.

No hatred now, only uneasiness at the memory. It wasn't in her nature to have sought any sort of vengeance, but since his back was to her, anyway, she took some. She screwed up her face and stuck out her tongue—just as he flipped a toggle switch, tossed the paper on the bench, and turned around.

She tried to remodel the childish gesture into a licking of her lips. Because of the glint that leaped into Owen's gray eyes, she wasn't sure she'd succeeded. He propped his lean backside against the workbench, folded his arms across his well-muscled chest, and coolly drawled, "Well, well, well."

His voice was like a feather pillow in the face, a small, painless shock. It was low, with a sandy quality that could be caustic or sensual as his moods shifted—and Owen was definitely a man of shifty moods. "Little Sara Dugan returns," he said, sardonic and almost whispering, and little Sara Dugan felt a shiver run down her spine.

In spite of the shiver and the memories, Sara's smile grew. "Little Sara Dugan's not so little anymore, and I don't know why you act like you didn't know I'd come home. I've seen you at church. You must have seen me."

That had always been ironic. Owen Dixon, the wild man, had always been a fairly regular member of her church's congregation. She couldn't count the number of times she'd heard the "grown-ups" debate whether a man who had earned himself the nickname Devil ought to be welcomed in their midst. She had heard none of that since coming back. Perhaps she hadn't been back long enough.

Owen's granite eyes made a quick tour of her upper body that would have insulted some women. It irritated Sara. He brought his eyes back to her face. A grin germinated. "Dadgum, lady, you're right. Sara's *not* so little anymore. I did see a gussied up blonde who looked something like little Sara Dugan. I didn't take her for you."

She wasn't sure if that was a compliment or not, so she ignored it and fell back on the conventions.

"How have you been, Owen?"

He looked at her for a full five seconds. "What do you want?"

The non sequitur, still in that slightly mocking voice, startled her.

"Pardon?"

"What . . . do . . . you . . . want, Sara?" He spoke with exaggerated slowness, as though she were mentally deficient. "You've acted like I had the black plague these last few years. Now you're hanging over my front counter asking after my welfare. What do you want?"

She knew what he meant. Halloween. He had never mentioned it, not once, nor had she. They had pretended, by mutual—at least she thought it had been mutual—unspoken consent, that Halloween hadn't happened. She stared at him with wide, hurt eyes for a moment before she made herself say, "One nice thing about you, Owen—you're never dull."

"That's one," he agreed. "Are you planning on being a customer, or am I supposed to stand around wasting time on polite socialisms? There's work to do."

There was a look in his eyes she had seen before, probably such a habit that he couldn't help himself.

Since he obviously wanted to cut to the bottom line, she swallowed and said, "I'm here about the job."

There. She had succeeded in surprising him. His black eyebrows rose into the wicked ridges that had helped give him his nickname, and he said, "Pardon me?"

She leaned her elbows on the high counter. "I came about the job you advertised in the *Roundup*."

He studied her, his eyes narrowed, his head cocked to one side. As always, Sara baffled him, though he'd never admit it. Sara was not tall, Sara was not muscular, and Sara was normally almost painfully shy, but around him, Sara often displayed an amazing inclination to behave like a mule. She'd speak in that hushed voice—a voice that sounded like it belonged to some sultry blond bombshell, not little Sara Dugan—and that hushed little voice could impale a man's soul as well as any deep, nasty baritone.

Owen straightened out of his slouch against the bench and advanced to the sales counter. A note lay beside the register. He popped the cash drawer open, put the paper inside, then shut the drawer with a precise click.

Sara was entertained. *Thinking. Stalling for time, thinking what to say now, how to send me off without inviting a discrimination suit, what a royal pain I'd be as an employee.* She could almost hear the gears turn.

After a moment, he moved opposite her, leaned his palms on the counter so that he was a couple of feet away, and looked down into her soft brown eyes with his direct gray ones. The shiver scuttled down her back again, and up into her middle where it turned hot and liquid. Being this close to Owen again made her knees go slightly weak.

"You're not serious, are you?" he breathed after a moment. "About the job?"

"I certainly am," she said firmly, in spite of lacking breath. "You haven't hired anyone else, have you?"

He shook his head slightly. "I'm trying to figure what rich little Sara Dugan wants with a pathetic, temporary, part-time job in a hat shop."

"Money. You surely didn't think I came for the company."

His eyes narrowed. Fascinated, she watched a grin creep across his face, lighting it handsomely. *No wonder he could always have any woman he wanted.*

"What," he persisted, still wearing the grin, "does rich little Sara Dugan want with money?"

"Oh, to buy food, clothing, and shelter. Just the necessities—I have all the diamonds, yachts, and race horses I want."

"You gonna try to tell me your daddy didn't drop dead last year and leave you a tidy bundle?"

"You're so—tactful and compassionate. No," she said patiently. "That's half true. It was a tiny bundle—an uncomplicated insurance policy, split between Robert and me. The interest on my half wouldn't feed a cat. I have three choices. One—I can go on as I am, semi-sponging off my brother—"

"He can afford it."

Robert was a veterinarian with a decent large-animal practice, but he was not rich.

"That's beside the point. I don't like mooching off him. I don't like sharing a house with him, either. Two—I can draw on the principal, in which case I'll have nothing at all in a couple of years. Three—I can bring in some extra money to supplement the interest. Which would you choose?"

"Oh, you know me," he drawled. "I'd take the principal out, spend it on a couple of perverted women, then accidentally shoot myself in the knee and collect disability for the rest of my life."

"Owen!" Sara was half amused and half disgusted. "That's a terrible thing to say!"

"It's what people'd expect, isn't it?"

"Since when do you do what people expect?"

"No oftener than I can help." The grin flashed again, shooting another tremble into Sara's middle. "You don't want to work for me."

"I could have sworn I did." She looked up at him seriously. "I need the job, Owen. Really do."

"There're other jobs."

"Not many." She straightened away from the counter. "The economy's slow all over Arizona, but you know what it's like up here in the off-season—even worse. I thought it would be nice to work for—a friend. I could probably get a job in one of the fast-food restaurants, but I'd rather do something I'm at least interested in."

He gave a soft snort. She knew exactly what he meant. Her hips attested to her interest in food. She ignored the snipe.

"I've been hunting something full-time, with no luck. Temporary jobs could get me through until I can get something permanent. I'm a good secretary, you know."

An extra alertness came into his eyes. "Are you, now?"

"What, you thought I was sitting around, nursing Daddy and enjoying the balmy one-hundred-twenty-two-degree Phoenix summer days? I attended business school and got me some learnin'. I also had a job down there these past two years, until the economy struck and half of America and I were laid off." She reached for the envelope. "It's all here. My résumé and letters of recommendation. I'm probably overqualified, but don't worry that I'll feel unfulfilled. It's temporary. Frankly, I think this sounds much more interesting than hustling fast food."

"Do you?" There was a faint challenge in that. "You don't know anything about it."

"Only because you've kept it a deep, dark secret, so far." She tried a smile.

The smile bounced harmlessly off him. His eyes traveled down to the envelope on the counter. He didn't look inside it as she wanted him to. Instead, he drilled her with his cool gray eyes and said, "Bookkeeping. Letters. Nothing fancy, but the old-fashioned way— there's no computer and no typewriter in this shop. I want somebody to handle phone calls and learn to write up orders. Lots of backed-up paperwork needs doing, but it won't last long."

She shrugged. "A minute here is better than two months at Zippy Burger. Sounds simple enough. I can handle it."

"Think so?" was all he said, with that mocking little smile playing around his mouth. His eyes examined her face closely, making her faintly uncomfortable. Maybe the rain had smeared her makeup or her hair was mussed from her hat. There were three good mirrors in the room—one of them hanging crookedly—but she hadn't had the sense to check her face. . . . Under his inspection, she felt like running from the room. She forced herself to say, calmly, "I've missed you, Owen."

"That's real sweet. What'd you say your name was again?"

One way of dealing with Owen's little vagaries was to ignore them. "If you don't mind my asking, why are you hiring?"

His scrutiny seemed to have settled in the vicinity of her mouth, and instead of waiting for his reply, she said sharply, *"Quit it!"*

His eyes came up slowly to meet hers, and she saw a small spurt of glee leap to life in them. "Quit what?"

"Owen, you know! It's one of your stupid games. One of your *tests*. After a couple of minutes, a woman's supposed to either run screaming into the night or jump into bed with you. I've seen you do it a thousand times!"

He moved his hands farther apart on the counter so

that he leaned closer to her and breathed near her cheek, "A thousand times?"

She could smell his after-shave. Woodsy, clean, and familiar. *What is it?* she almost asked, but caught herself just in time. He would have enjoyed that question immensely.

"All right. Thirty. I've seen you do it thirty times, then. Quit trying to do it to me. It doesn't work!"

He grinned and lounged back from the counter to lean against the workbench again, this time with his thumbs hooked in his Levi's pockets. "It never did. Way back, I thought it was because I hadn't perfected it yet, but it still doesn't. Guess you've got a natural immunity."

"Thank God." She smiled shyly and pushed the envelope forward. "Please look at this. Check my references. You didn't tell me why you want to hire someone. You never have before. I asked. Nobody can remember your grandfather having anyone work for him, either, except you, and that wasn't work."

"I beg your pardon, lady. I worked blamed hard for my grandfather."

"You didn't get paid money for it." Her gesture encompassed the entire shop. "This is your pay. He left it to you because he knew you were the only one of the family that cared about it. Anyway, why do you need someone to work for you?"

He studied her face again. It was a friendlier study, now that he had dropped that piercing sexy-eye routine of his. She bore it patiently, until he asked, "Have you actually had success handling job interviews this way?"

"This isn't an interview. This is a conversation. Very one-sided, too. Why are you hiring, Owen? Is it some big secret? Did you get a government contract for night-vision cowboy hats or something?"

He came away from the workbench, moving easily around the end of the counter. Sara had mixed emotions about that. She wanted to be closer to him—maybe that hug could still be worked out—and yet the counter had provided some decent insulation.

"That's not a bad idea. Least, it wouldn't have been in the old days, for nighthawk riders. No government contract, but something interesting." He hesitated. "I'll tell you about it, little Sara, if you'll swear you won't tell anybody else, including family and ardent admirers."

"No problem. I never confide in my family unless I want the world to know, and my admirers are so ardent we don't waste time talking about such things."

His grin said he didn't buy that for a second.

"I promise I won't say anything about it," she said, "whatever *it* may be."

He chewed on the inside of his lip for a moment, watching her. He had known Sara for a long time. He'd bedeviled her for years. She usually accepted his little attacks calmly, with an irritating sort of quiet rebuke that left him feeling mildly guilty but not guilty enough to stop. She offered, he accepted. She gave, he took. That had been their relationship. They had talked lightly, rather than shared deep secrets. They had never dated or been in each other's family home. He had never been quite sure what it was that made her keep coming back, but in some intrinsic way he had always been glad she did. He was glad now, even relieved. There was something restful about Sara. She didn't play games. Shy as she had always been, she always had the gumption to stand up to him when he prodded her. He knew a lot of men he couldn't say that of. He had missed her more than he had realized.

Could he trust her? Logic said no. Instinct said yes. He had told no one about this deal. He hadn't had the faintest desire, until now, to tell anyone about it. He didn't know why, but, like old times, every instinct goaded him to share it with Sara.

She was squirming under his long regard. With a

smile that had nothing to do with what he was about to say, he moved closer. He liked to push into her personal space, just to see how far he could go. It was entertaining to watch her back off at the last minute, a little afraid of him.

This time was different. She let him come quite close, within touching distance. He noted it in the back of his mind as he asked, "Heard of Maddox Western Stores?"

"Sure. There must be three or four in the Phoenix area."

Small lights bounced in her hair when she nodded. Owen's hand seemed to have a strong, independent desire to reach out and smooth a loose tendril back behind her ear. When had Sara turned into such an attractive young lady, anyway?

Hands off. She was too young. He liked his women with a little more know-how under their skirts. He leaned a hip against the counter and folded his arms.

"Yeah. There's one in Tucson, and others in Albuquerque, Denver, and—Casper, Wyoming, I think. They've done well."

"I didn't realize they were so big." Her eyes widened. "Owen! Do they want you to make a line of hats for them? They *do*!" she exclaimed softly. "I knew someone was bound to someday."

He grinned crookedly. "Keep rubbin' that butter on, honey. It feels real good."

"You're talented. I've always thought it a shame that you're so far off the beaten path."

"Believe me, I'm as near the beaten path as I want to be. Anyway, that's not what they want."

Her forehead crinkled in a frown. "What, then?"

He hesitated. He had seen simultaneous flashes of joy and regret in her eyes when she'd thought he was going to go big-time. What would she think when she heard the truth?

"They're interested in buying the shop."

She gasped, a sharp, inhaled, *"Ah!"*

"That," he said, "is the kind of sound folks make when they see a terrible car accident."

She stood a moment longer with her mouth ajar. "I can't believe it."

"Fact."

"What would they want a place like this for?"

"Thank you."

"You know what I mean." Her nose wrinkled as she added, "Maddox stores are big, jazzy places, nothing like this . . ."

"Shabby, run-down hole?"

She heard a touch of anger in his voice. She reached out and lightly touched his sleeve. "I was going to say homey. Comfortable. Owen, you aren't thinking of selling it to them, are you?"

He cocked a challenging eyebrow. "I may."

"I don't understand." She realized her fingertip had begun rubbing his flannel sleeve. She pulled her hand back. "This isn't their kind of store. Why would they want it? It's not big enough—they'd have to knock out a wall and add something. They'd probably put in fluorescent lights."

Owen winced.

"Sorry," she said. "Do you know what they're thinking? Because I can't imagine."

He pushed up his hat, rubbed his forehead where the sweatband had been, then resettled the hat. "Yeah, I know what they're thinking. I had a call from Bentin Maddox a couple weeks ago—that's how all this came up. The Maddoxes went into the mail-order business a while back, like a couple other good-sized Western-wear stores have done. It's been pretty successful. They're looking to try something different, an experiment."

"Like what?"

"Like—a catalog store."

She wrinkled her nose again. It was so cute he nearly bent down and kissed it, which would have sent her scuttling for cover and blasted the entire conversation. "You mean," she said, "like Sears?"

"Something like. A small stock of seasonal merchandise that will sell well locally, and an order desk where customers can order what they can't buy on site. Maddox says they've done some surveys in small towns, and their customers like the idea. He says this is exactly the sort of place they're hunting for to try it out."

Sara looked around the familiar, homelike room with its population of felt mushrooms. She could almost see Benjamin Dixon behind the cash register, swearing—quietly, because a young lady was present—because the drawer wouldn't open.

"Let me bust it open, Granddad," Owen had said.

"No," the old man had insisted stubbornly. *"When I'm dead and gone, do whatever you want with it. Now leave it to me."*

She brought her eyes around to Owen's and said softly, "You can't sell it. Your grandfather—"

"Is *dead*." He spoke sharply and unfolded his arms, suddenly nine feet tall. "He's been dead for years."

Like a little boy, she thought around another of those peculiar skips in her heart rate, on the defensive because someone touched a wound.

"I know," she said gently. She saw the muscles in his jaw work then ease. He settled back, relaxing. His temper, like a drop of water slung on a hot grill, usually danced and sizzled and, in a moment, was gone. She said, "I think I never told you how sorry I was when he died."

"You did. I don't remember where, exactly. I remember you did. I remember there being—" The memory assaulted him, grabbing his throat and squeezing it.

"I remember there being tears in those big eyes of yours."

Sara shifted uncomfortably. "My eyes aren't any bigger than anyone else's."

"Yes, they are. With lashes like this." He put his fingers up in front of his eyes and wriggled them at her.

She grinned, embarrassed by the left-handed compliment, and lowered her eyes, suddenly conscious of the feel of lashes she had always considered stubby. "He was a nice man," she said, reverting to their former subject.

"He was a mean old rascal. I never knew him to just up and laugh at anything."

"He was good to you."

"We never went hungry," he allowed. "That's water under the bridge. He's not here now, and the decision's mine."

"What does Haddon think?"

"Haddon? I don't give a rat's hind end what Haddon thinks. Far as he's concerned, if it don't have four legs and whinny, it ain't worth considerin'. Pity the woman ever falls in love with him." At her questioning look, he continued. "Grandad didn't leave this place to Drew—he was already off in Denver being Super Cop. He didn't leave it to Haddon because he knew Haddon's calling was horses. He left it to me because he knew I had no calling but cared something for it, and he was sure my life would go straight to hell without it. *Therefore*, it has done its job. My life has not gone and is not going straight to hell. I think if he were here he'd see the sense in considering Maddox's offer."

Sara felt chilly suddenly; she hugged herself. "If you sold it—what would you do?"

"Don't know. That's part of the considering, isn't it?"

She searched his eyes for some sign of hope or happiness at the prospect of the sale. She saw nothing but distant gray steel. If the shop were sold, would he open another, or would he acquire a new trade? Would he stay in Payson, or go elsewhere, leaving her behind? He must not have minded her absence these last years— he'd made no effort to contact her. If his life changed so radically, would he find there was no longer the tiniest space in it for little Sara? Would he finally find space for some other woman? The thought made her heart constrict stupidly. She had no claim on him. He *ought* to have someone, she told herself. He shouldn't be alone.

". . . looking at Christmas orders, which I could normally fill by just not goofing off, plus whatever ev-er'day orders come along. There are always folks who come, last minute, and fall at my boots, promising un-dying devotion if I'll get their husband/brother/boy-friend/father's hat done by Christmas Eve."

Women nuzzling his boots was what he meant. She tried not to look irritated.

Owen continued, "I'm already behind on paperwork— it not being my favorite chore. I looked into the future and saw the bookkeeping going to pot while I do hats. Happens every year; takes me two months to catch up. I ought to have things in the kind of order to fetch the best price. When Maddox comes, I want everything caught up and polished to a fare-thee-well. That's why I'm hiring."

"When's he coming?"

"I just told you," he said with synthetic kindness, "he's coming up at Christmas to ski at Sunrise if the snow's decent. That gives me about three weeks to get things under control."

"Why don't you want anyone to know about this? It should be good for the shop's reputation."

"Maddox asked me to keep it quiet. I reckon he doesn't want anybody else getting the idea the place is up for grabs. I don't want it talked around. I like things quiet. I want them kept quiet. Time to make a fuss if and when there's a sale."

Imagine, Devil Dixon saying he liked things *quiet*.

"Do you know anything about these Maddoxes? I mean, are they honest people to deal with?"

"Far as I know. I've seen them written up in the trade journals a couple of times. They sound all right." He saw her eyebrows go up when he mentioned the journals. "I can read, you know."

"Why, yes, I know, Owen," she said demurely. "I simply didn't realize you read things that came without a centerfold."

His chuckle sounded loud in the silence of the shop. "Why, little Sara, the things you think!" He laughed again, looking at her as if she were some unique creature in a zoo. "Why don't you get out of here, now, and let me get back to work?"

"All right. When do I start?"

"Start what?"

"The job. I'm going to take it."

She saw something all at once puzzled and defiant in his eyes as he said, "I don't remember offering it to you."

That was a smack in the face, the way he said it, with a kind of gentle contempt. Her heart thudding dully, she lifted her chin. "I want it, Owen. I don't mean to sound like I'm barging in and jerking it away from you, but I want it. I want you to know how much I want it."

"You don't even know what it pays."

"What does it pay?"

"Minimum wage."

"Owen!" Images of hot, greasy grills and rainy drive-through windows subdued her immediately. "Okay— I'll make you a deal."

Tolerant amusement appeared in his eyes. "I don't think you're in any position to deal."

"The deal is," she continued doggedly, "I work for you now, for minimum wage—paid *weekly*—and, when the work's done, you'll teach me how to be a hatter."

His dark eyebrows winged up again, and she knew he couldn't decide whether to laugh or unceremoniously heave her out into the rain. He stuck one finger in his ear and jiggled it. "I could have sworn I heard you say—no, I must have imagined it."

"I mean it. I want you to teach me to make hats."

"What for? You've got a decent trade. You went to *business* school."

"It's a good trade, but yours is a craft!"

"What're you gonna do, open a shop across the highway and go into competition with me? Good luck."

"I don't know. Maybe I'll never get the chance to use it practically, but once I've learned it, I'll know something few people know, and I like that idea. Besides, if you sell out and run away and join a circus or something, who'll be left? I want you to do it."

"Excuse me. I must be extra stupid today. I keep lookin' for the benefit for me in this *deal*, and, so help me, I don't see it. What's in it for me, other than a prolonged pain in the—neck?"

Unfortunately, he was right. There wasn't anything in The Deal for anybody but Sara. She cleared her throat. "Well—there'd be someone local, skilled in the trade, upon whom you could call in case of emergency."

"For instance?"

"For instance," she supplied with a gritty note, "if some crazed husband broke both your arms."

He shoved his hat back and gave an appreciative hoot of laughter that was either infectious or insulting, she couldn't decide which.

"It's not that funny."

"It's funnier than you know."

"Owen?"

His grin died. He looked at her a long time while his thumb stroked absently back and forth on the wood of the countertop, and she could not tell what he was thinking.

"What do you know about making hats, little Sara?"

"Not much," she admitted. "What I've learned from watching your grandfather and you. I know they're made of felt or straw, and I know the difference between a crown and a brim. I love the way they look and smell. Everybody has to start somewhere."

He gave a short laugh—more of a snicker, really—and said, "I've got people interviewing for the job this afternoon and tomorrow. You know—people who called and made *appointments* the conventional way?"

"I'm sorry," she said, feeling The Deal slipping away. "I know I should've done that. I was so excited when I saw your ad, I didn't want to waste a second. I was afraid you'd give the job to somebody else before I got here. I'm good. You won't be sorry."

The gleam in his eyes turned positively wicked. "I'm sure you're good, little Sara. We'll see."

"Shall I check with you tomorrow?"

"I'll call you."

Sara shrugged into her jacket. "When?"

"When I've made up my mind."

She jammed her rain hat down on her head.

"My number's on my résumé."

"I'll cherish it till death."

"How long will it take you to make up your mind?"

"As long as it takes!"

His tone menaced, but she grinned. "Okay. Guess I'll—wait to hear from you, then."

"You do that little thing."

She had to walk between him and a dry sink with hats hooked over the ears of its splash board. As she did so, his fingers caught her arm—just his fingers, lingering and sending warm pulses of energy through her sweater. Startled, she looked up at his face, so close she could see the texture of his skin.

"I'm glad you're back, little Sara." It was pitched low, almost a whisper. "Doggone if I didn't miss you."

Owen Dixon expressing rank sentimentalism? She was shocked, touched, and a trifle angry. She wondered if he could feel her body tremble, or if the trembling was only some sort of internal illusion.

"Really? That's interesting. If you missed me so much, how come you never called me?"

"Ouch." He winced slightly. There wasn't much, if any, regret in his eyes, only amusement. "How 'bout— I didn't know where you were?"

"Robert knew."

"So he did. How 'bout—my dialing finger was broke?"

"An operator could have assisted you."

She wasn't backing down. She probed him with those brown doe eyes and he felt unusually guilty. How could you tell a girl who had been a decent friend that the distance between them had been a good thing? How could you tell her she'd grown into something that made your mouth water when she came near? How could you warn her off of yourself for her own good, and make her believe it? He hadn't been able to do it when she was an awkward eighteen; it wasn't any easier when she was twenty-three and filled out in all the right directions. *Think fast.*

He shoved his hat forward and rubbed the back of his head. "How 'bout—you'd made it pretty plain you wanted some distance between us. Maybe I figured a little more distance was a good thing."

Her eyes widened. She hesitated, then asked, "Why would you think I wanted distance between us?"

"I'm not stupid." He raised an eyebrow. "After that night, you kept six feet between us to talk. If I touched you, you jumped like a maggot'd crawled up your pants leg." His eyes mocked. "You never wanted to go anywhere with me again. Can't say I blame you much."

She knew he was talking about that dark Halloween. They had given each other plenty of space, all right, after that night. A peculiar friendship they'd had, cemented by little more than instinct and a queer chemistry.

She raised her chin, her eyes tracing the clean lines of his face. There was no way she could help but smile shyly up at him. "Well . . . I had a terrible crush on you in the old days. You know?"

"I know." There was a laugh in his voice, and his eyes were arrogant.

"I finally reached a point where I opened my eyes and saw you had all the grown-up women you could want close at hand, and you couldn't possibly appreciate a teeny-bopper trotting at your heels, so I quit. It was rather—embarrassing, actually."

His smile was quizzical. "I don't know what your definition of a teeny-bopper is. You never fit mine."

She shrugged slightly. "Guess it doesn't matter now. I hope I've grown out of that."

"I hope so, too," he said with feeling, and, again, she smiled up from under her lashes. "I meant it when I said I missed having you around, though. Habit, I 'spect."

"There's a compliment in there somewhere, I feel sure," she said gamely. "I'll find it eventually. . . . I missed you, too. A lot."

"Yeah? Then how come you didn't call me?"

"Touché." She said it ruefully. "It—all happened quickly. The doctor said go, Robert made a couple of phone calls, and we went. I nearly went nuts trying to get things ready for the movers. I'd never had to coordinate something like that before. . . . I tried to call you.

There was never any answer. You should get a machine.''

"Hate 'em.''

"I did try—'' She broke off, wanting to look away but finding her eyes hooked on his.

"You did try?'' he prodded.

"I did look for you, the night before we left. . . .'' His eyes mercilessly dragged the rest out of her. "You were at the Rim Shot with . . . people.''

"You mean you came in there?''

"Yes.''

"And you didn't say good-bye?''

She stirred uncomfortably, still scalded by the sight of him perched on a bar stool with his left hand curled around a fistful of popcorn and his right arm curled around the waist of a slim blond girl. Their heads had been close together; they had been laughing. It hadn't been a surprise, it had just been the last of many blows.

"You were busy.''

Owen remembered that night, too. Later he had wondered if Sara might have tried calling him while he'd been busy making time with . . . some yellow-haired wench named Starlight or Moonbeam or some other weird Earth Mother name, who'd taken a fancy to him that night. He'd beaten her off with a stick and gone home hungry, and the next day Robert had dropped in and said, "Sara moved down to the Valley with Dad. She said 'so long.' ''

They stood looking at each other for a long, silent moment, while the rain pattered on the roof. Sara felt Owen's presence now, as she always had, as a peculiar tugging at her senses. He smelled wonderful, like pine smoke, felt, and man. At such times, she willed him with all her might to reach out and draw her to him. It never worked. Telepathy was a joke.

"I'm sorry about your daddy,'' Owen said gently. "You know I liked him.''

Her throat tightened. She nodded. "He liked you, too. He always stuck up for you when the church board fussed."

"Maybe it runs in the family, then. Sara, you are the strangest little friend a man ever—"

The brasses jingled. Intent on each other, they hadn't heard a car drive up. Owen pulled his hand back as if he'd put it in a flame, and Sara passed by him toward the tunnel.

"Call and let me know."

"Yeah," Owen said behind her.

The customers were tourists, a couple with heavy Scottish accents, hunting something unusual and dry. She smiled at them, once they had emerged from the tunnel, and went out into the freshly laundered day.

She walked down the short, pine-flanked drive that led to the highway where her brother would pick her up. Panting slightly, more from shaken nerves than from exertion, she was grateful for the cool, piny air.

It had not gone too badly. There had been less acid in the teasing she had endured than there would have been four years ago. Robert had said Owen had mellowed. He might be right.

What an odd thing Owen had just said, though, calling her a strange little friend. He had never seemed to have real friends, just the wild young men he'd hung out with and the long string of women who had been attached to him. In spite of that—or maybe because of that—she had always thought of herself as Owen's friend. He had treated her more gently than he had the others. Even when, after that awful Halloween, she had kept a self-protective distance between them, it had seemed the most natural thing to understand and still be Owen's friend.

What had happened between them just now? Owen had surely wanted to do more than just touch her sleeve. She might have wangled that imagined hug. She might, she thought with a rueful, twisted smile, have wangled that imagined kiss. . . .

Owen did what he wanted to do, everyone knew that. If he had wanted to do more, he would have done it.

Owen had gone behind the counter and taken up the pouncing paper again. The tourists were more interested in the antiques than the hats, something he was used to. It was always a blow to their acquisitive souls when he told them the antiques were only for display purposes, not for sale. He started the wheel and bent to the hat.

Little Sara Dugan had the annoying habit of being right too often. He did test women because it sorted them into one of two types, so he knew where he stood.

Type One didn't often run screaming into the night, but she did generally dissolve into nervous jelly or become annoyed at the boldness of his eyes, and give him a wide berth, which was fine with him. Women who simpered or played coy were a waste of time. A woman without a sense of adventure, or at least, humor, annoyed him.

Type Two passed the first test and was ready for the next, the more intimate variety that ordinarily was given between bed sheets. Some of them even had to take the advanced exams more than once. Some had come really close, but nobody had ever passed.

Sara was the only woman who'd ever just looked him in the face and said "Quit it!" She didn't fail the tests. She just didn't participate. She laughed at or dodged them, lowering her long eyelashes to hide her response and forged right on. Maybe that, even more than his own raw, freshly discovered weakness and misery, had goaded him into blind-siding her in the schoolyard at that juvenile Halloween party and rushing her into the darkness before she could scream or use her knee on him. In fact, he didn't doubt she'd been too innocent to know she should use her knee on him. Lucky.

He had laughed, at first. She had laughed, too. He always remembered, with a sharp rush of exquisite pleasure, the smell of her short hair and the delicate texture of her throat beneath his mouth and, once his hand had found its way inside her stupid green frog costume, the nuzzling of the hardened tip of her small, warm, satin breast into his palm.

Then always came the other rush of memory. Through a fog of misery and lust, he had realized the moans coming from her throat were not of pleasure. He remembered the overwhelming humiliation that had radiated from her, threatening to smother him even as Haddon had materialized out of the darkness, like an avenging angel, before Owen had had a chance to calm her, to apologize, to ease her terror. . . .

He remembered that night every time he saw Sara Dugan. Always, when he spoke to her, he was a breath away from apologizing, but he never did. Always he wondered if she looked at him and remembered, too. Always he wondered if she ever lay in bed at night, aching in body and soul, remembering that night.

He wouldn't hire her. Having a genuine secretary look after the paperwork during the holidays would take a worry off his mind, but having Sara in the shop would be the worst kind of masochism. If any of the other applicants could read and write—maybe just read *or* write—he would hire her instead. Sara was grown up and lovely, but every bit of sense he had told him to steer clear of her.

He returned to the workbench with a last look around the quiet room, at the Scots oohing over the Duke Hat, the mirrors, and the sentinel hats and shadows. He didn't believe in ghosts, but there were times when he could feel his grandfather's silent, rebuking presence. He said firmly but under his breath, "She's not working here," and bent over the waltzing hat.

TWO

It was days before the phone interrupted Sara's breakfast.

Owen asked, "Still want the job?"

"What do you think?"

"I think I've lost my mind. . . . Understand, if I hire you, there're no promises about teaching you anything except how to make coffee the way I like it."

Sara scarcely had to consider. There was always a chance she could make him change his mind. If not, she would still earn some money at an interesting, if brief, job. "I can live with that."

There was a short silence, then Owen said gruffly, "I might throw in lunch a couple times a week, if things work out right."

Surprised, she said, "That would be nice of you, Owen."

"When could you start?"

"Now," she said promptly. "Give me ten minutes to get dressed and five to get to the shop."

She could hear his grin. "Sara, it's Sunday."

"I forgot," she said sheepishly. "I could start tomorrow."

"How many hours a week would you be able to give me?"

"As many as you want."

"I reckon fifteen or twenty, anyway."

"Owen, I'll give you whatever you want."

He gave a little sigh. "*Mercy*, if only more women would say that. Okay. Tomorrow morning."

"I'm looking forward to it. You won't be sorry!" She was practically dancing in the kitchen. "What do you want me to wear?"

"Personally, I'd like something satin—red, maybe, with black lace, and net stockings—but jeans will do. Eight o'clock. Don't be late."

"I'll be there before eight!"

"Then you'll be standin' in the cold 'til I get there."

"Owen? Thank—"

He had already hung up.

Sara had to admit, later, that she had approached the job with the wrong attitude, with visions of stashes of unposted receipts, unpaid bills, and unanswered correspondence to be organized and updated by Sara Dugan, Super Secretary. It wasn't that she thought Owen was sloppy. She simply saw him as a man with other priorities. Lots of other priorities.

She walked in that morning, pleased to be part of that pleasant place, however temporarily. Her hair was down, long and loose; she'd worn jeans, a soft blue-striped rugby shirt, and loafers, instead of red satin. The idea of wearing red satin for Owen had produced some interesting, hard-to-banish mental images.

Owen was putting the cash in the register. She said, "Good morning!" and instead of returning the greeting, he looked up from the money with a feeling of fatalistic foreboding. Why hadn't he just climbed a tall building and jumped off? Pinning her with his gray eyes, he said, "What's that?"

She glanced down at her load. "It's a typewriter," she said kindly. "You must have heard of them. Invented over a hundred years ago."

"Get it out of here." She thought he was joking until his eyes came up as his hands pushed the drawer shut and he said, "I don't want that thing in here."

She rested the typewriter on the seat of the stove chair. "Why?"

"I don't want to listen to it."

"It's a smooth electronic machine, not like the old clattery electrics."

"I don't care if it only pantomimes, I don't want it in here. You don't need it."

"You said I'd be doing correspondence."

"You will."

"You surely don't mean for me to write by hand!"

"I surely do."

"But—"

He was doing things behind the counter, bending out of sight one minute, straightening and turning his back the next, making it impossible to read his eyes. She had the feeling he wanted it that way.

Sara said reasonably, "You know, I'm a fast, accurate typist. I can give you professional correspondence in so much less time—"

"I don't want professional correspondence."

Confused, she murmured, "Why?"

"What I want is personal correspondence." He turned from the workbench. "The orders get written by hand, the letters get written by hand, the envelopes get addressed by hand, and the hats get made by hand. It's what my customers like. Some of them are old-timers, customers of my grandfather's. They don't feel like a piece of data in a machine, that way. It's that simple. It's worked for a long time, and that's how it's going to be as long as I have anything to say about it, which brings me to another reason: Because I Said So. Now eighty-six that thing and I'll show you where you're going to work.''

Well—Owen had a bee in his bonnet this morning. She said quietly, "I don't know a lot about this kind of thing, but when Mr. Maddox comes, it seems to me he's going to want to see certain things."

"Such as?"

"Such as financial statements. Profit and Loss. Balance sheets. Do you actually want to show him handwritten statements? Don't," she added as his mouth opened, "say it's what your grandfather would have done. I think he would have had someone type them for him so he wouldn't look clumsy."

He gave the typewriter a long look of loathing. "You're right," he admitted reluctantly. "Okay, but no correspondence."

"Unless it's something connected with the sale?"

"The *possible* sale."

"The possible sale."

"Okay," he allowed again, giving her a long look of frustration that she felt had little to do with the current discussion. "I hate it, but okay."

They spent a couple of minutes discussing her schedule. When they'd settled on five mornings a week, Owen led the way into the back room.

Instead of the chaos she had expected, she found a large pigeonhole desk with a bank of shelves rising up above it. Ledgers, stationery, catalogs, and books occupied most of the shelves. The pigeonholes held small supplies in neat order.

Another workbench ran the whole length of one wall. Odd-looking equipment—some of it resembling that on the workbench out front—squatted at one end, and shipping supplies occupied the other. Above it, tools, some as common as pliers and others more strange, hung in tidy rows. The minimal space was utilized efficiently. Apparently Owen, like his grandfather, believed in the axiom "a place for everything and everything in its place."

A heavily stuffed chair slouched near the single window, a blue plaid stadium blanket tossed over the back. It was easy to imagine old Benjamin reclining there, napping, maybe, with a young Owen at the bench.

A tiny bathroom was squeezed into one corner. Cavernous, cedar-lined cupboards for supplies and hats were on the remaining wall.

"These," she remarked when Owen swung the cupboard doors open to reveal a small stock of unstyled felt, "remind me of the hillbilly hats in the movies and in old photographs—kind of peaked, with the brim sloping down all around."

"It's called a 'body' or a 'cone.'" The bodies were nested like drinking glasses; Owen separated a chocolate-brown one and turned it between his hands. "At the factory, they spray a liquid mixture of furs onto a wire frame and produce this thing. Maybe the hill people were so poor they couldn't afford to buy a styled body. Maybe it was just something they liked."

"I thought you made your hats from scratch. You said this is made in a factory."

"Next, I'll take you out back and show you my pet beaver. Whenever I'm ready to start a hat, I grab him by the scruff of the neck and shave him naked."

She grinned. "I'm not really that ignorant. When you said your hats are handmade, I imagined that meant from the fur up, so to speak. . . . Do animal rights groups drive you crazy?"

"Over the fur in felt?" He shrugged. "Not much. I don't think most people think about fur in felt. I had one guy come in to order an old-fashioned Tom Mix–style hat. He talked a lot about his own animal rights group. I don't think it ever occurred to him he was ordering a beaver's best suit. I wasn't going to tell him."

"Doesn't it bother you?"

He didn't reply for a moment. "I wouldn't go out and shoot a beaver to see it die, but it serves a purpose, just as much as cows putting beef on the table. If people can't start farming beaver, I give beaver-fur felts another ten years. Then we'll make them of something else. We're using more rabbit all the time. The hats will never be as good, but they can be all right if they're made right. . . . What else are we going to use if not fur? Plastic? Somebody will scream it's a waste of petroleum product and fills up landfills. Paper? It's a waste of trees. We need to learn to make hats out of dirt. There's plenty of that."

He put the chocolate body back with the others and turned to the desk. "Everything you need is here. Journals. Addresses. Writing paper. Poke around, then I'll tell you what I want you to do first."

She poked. Two wooden file boxes held meticulous records of past customers. She saw two different styles of handwriting and realized the thin, spidery hand had belonged to Benjamin Dixon, while the larger, heavier, more precise hand was Owen's. Some cards bearing his grandfather's writing were yellowed and dated back more than forty years.

The books were orderly. The general ledger led to appropriate journals and Owen was not behind in posting. A cursory glance showed her he faithfully followed basic bookkeeping rules. Aware that she was guilty of stereotyping, Sara was surprised that a man who had grown up under the nickname Devil was so meticulous and mindful of the rules, down to and including no erasures or white-outs.

She was sitting in the old, leather swivel chair that must have served Owen's grandfather for many years, exploring the desk drawers, when Owen came and stood beside her.

"How you doin'?"

"Everything looks straightforward."

"Good. First thing, I need you to send out brochures." He took a small box from a shelf. "These letters asking for information have accumulated." He put one hand on the desktop, beside her, and leaned across, touching the appropriate pigeonholes as he spoke. "Brochures are here, price lists, and envelopes. Stationery up above. Stamps in the top drawer, left."

As he leaned nearer, every nerve in Sara's body suddenly went on red alert. Her skin warmed and tightened up, reaching out sensitive, invisible fingers toward him, as if to meet similar invisible fingers of his own. She stole a look up at him.

Calm. Normal. Whatever was affecting her had not touched Owen.

"Get familiar with the brochure and price list, then read each letter. If they want general information, send a brochure and price list. If they've asked a question the brochure doesn't answer, write them a note. I'll sign it."

"I can sign and initial it. It's a standard business practice. That way I won't have to bother you."

"Bother me. You understand what I want you to do?"

She had followed his pointing finger and his words and found them quite explanatory. She looked up at him, mildly insulted.

"If you're going to tell me how much quicker and easier this would be with a typewriter, forget it," he said, having read her mind. "And don't," he added with his vexing grin, "use red ink, little Sara."

He went back into the shop. Sara was left savoring the faint, lingering scent of his woodsy shaving lotion and with the faint, lingering feeling that he thought she was three years old. He'd called her little Sara for as long as she had known him, and it had never bothered

her before, but it was starting to. It was definitely starting to.

She read and wrote notes for half an hour before
Owen came back.

He said, "If there's anything you don't understand,
ask."

She said she would.

Fifteen minutes later, he was back. "When you're
through with that, you can start updating the ledger.
Receipts, vouchers, invoices, and so forth, are in these
envelopes." His explanatory finger again touched a
pigeonhole.

"I saw them. Thanks."

The third time, he took a hat to the corner where the
odd-looking machines sat on the long bench. From
the corner of her eye, she saw the hat go into one of the
gadgets upside down. There was a sudden soft hissing,
and steam flooded out in a thin cloud that floated up
and over Owen's shoulder.

Owen heard the chair give a creak as she turned. He
said, "Sorry. You'll have to get used to my coming
and going."

"It won't bother me. I just wondered what you're
doing."

"Flanging the brim—making it as smooth and symmetrical as possible."

"May I come and watch?"

"No. You may correspond your brains out, though."

Twenty minutes later, she went out to where Owen
was perched on the stool at the workbench. He had a
black hat upside down between his knees and was pulling a needle and thread out of it.

"Oh, *that's* fascinating," she observed, grinning.

He glanced up. "Apparently, fascinating you don't
take a whole lot."

"Do people around here know you sew, Owen? Do
you do needlepoint, too? Little cotton frocks?"

He concentrated on sewing the lining into place inside the hat. He could hardly decide whether to ignore her sarcasm or get up and shake her.

She moved in for a closer look. His fingers were quick and sure, as if he had done the stitch a million times. She said, "You're very good at that."

"Honey," he said, with a quick glance and a brazen grin, "I'm very good at most ever'thing."

Her answering smile was wistful. He wasn't very good at making polite conversation, or letting people get to know him, or settling down with one particular girl. He had worked as a mechanic for nearly three years after graduating from high school, and everyone had said he could make an engine sing like no one else. He had rodeoed when he was younger and had been fairly good at that. He had done some stock car and motorcycle racing, too, and been good at that. There had been any number of women who thought he was "good." Apparently, he was even a good bookkeeper.

She fluttered a piece of stationery at him. "I hope you're good at explaining why you charge so much for a 10X hat. This man says he paid less for a 20X hat, and he thinks you're cheating your customers. Explanation, please: What is a 10X hat?"

He muttered something under his breath as he drew the needle out to the length of the thread, then said, "It's a system for rating felt quality. The more beaver fur, the better the quality—makes a lighter, denser, more pliable hat. The more rabbit fur, the coarser, more springy the hat. The more beaver, the more X's. It used to be standardized. A 10X was the finest hat, one hundred percent beaver. Nowadays, who knows? They're even using wool in real cheap hats—trashy stuff."

"So—it seems simple to me."

"Would be, if it weren't for hatmakers trying to make their product look better than everybody else's. They've trashed the old system and made up their own.

Now one manufacturer's best hat might be a 20X. Another's of the same quality, the same mixture of furs, is only 10X. A 5X hat used to be a decent midpriced hat, but there's no beaver fur at all anymore in any 5X hat.''

''How's a customer supposed to know what he's getting?''

''He's got to judge each hat on merit, look for a thin, pliable quality felt. As near as I can, I rate the old way. My top-quality hat is a 10X. That's one hundred percent beaver. I've seen 30X hats, so-called, come in here for cleaning. They're not a bit better than my 10X. You tell the man that. If he don't like it,'' he added softly, ''he can shove a cactus up his''—he tossed a wary look at her—''nose.''

''Thank you,'' she said dryly. ''I'll tell him. That should add a really *personal* touch.''

She started toward the back room but the phone by the cash register shrilled at her elbow and she snatched it.

'' 'Morning, Dixon Hat Company! . . . Yes, sir, we are. . . . Until five-thirty. . . . You're welcome.''

She hung up, feeling inanely proud of handling her first phone call, then caught Owen's eyes on her.

''Somebody wanting to know how late you're open.''

''I stay open until six.''

Owen watched her eyes widen. Beautiful, big brown eyes that had always poked him somewhere near his heart, filled now with growing outrage.

''Owen, the sign at the front door says five-thirty. I know it does! I made a point of looking at it when I came in this morning.''

He rotated the hat, easing the lining into a better position. ''The sign is wrong.''

''Then the sign should be changed.''

''The sign,'' he said with a note of warning, ''was

painted by my grandfather's own hands. The sign stays as it is.''

Sara had a sudden childish desire to punch him. "Then you should close at five-thirty. Or else get another sign, with an arrow pointing to the old sign, saying 'This sign—which is a family heirloom, and therefore inviolable—is just kidding. We're really open until six'!''

Her sarcasm only produced a surprisingly tolerant grin. "Get back in your cage.''

She sniffed and turned but paused and watched his hands take another deft stitch.

"Will you at least teach me to do that?''

He stopped and looked thoughtfully into the distance. "Oh, I don't know, little Sara. Can you sew? I mean, do you do needlepoint? Little cotton frocks?''

Ashamed of her earlier mockery, she said meekly, "I'm fairly good at embroidery.''

He went back to stitching. "Let's see how it goes.'' He gave his head a shake. "Maddox'll be here before you can shake a stick.''

"We'll do it,'' she assured him. She paused in the doorway. "Some of these letters mention an article in something called *Horse Source*. Was there an article about you somewhere?''

He fiddled with the hat before answering. "I let one of my customers interview me; he went and published it in *Horse Source*, complete with my address.''

"You don't sound happy about it. Free publicity.''

He shook his head, eyes still on the hat. "Most of those inquiries won't buy. They're curious. It's more trouble than it's worth.''

"Do you have a copy of the article I could see?''

"In the file cabinet, under *N*.''

"Okay . . . Why *N*?''

"For 'Nuisance.' '' He flashed her a sudden grin that

made her heart feel warm and mushy as she went back to the desk.

A short time later, he was bending over her again, saying, "I never did ask if you can make change."

She finished writing a line and looked up, immensely aware of the warmth of his big body next to hers. "Sure. Count from the smallest to the largest." She smiled suspiciously. "You never read my résumé, did you?"

"I skimmed it." He looked faintly self-conscious. "The other applicants were so pitiful there was no question about who was best qualified. I didn't need your résumé to know that. Keep an ear out for customers while I run to the bank for change."

There was a moment's first-day panic in Sara's stomach. "Okay, but if a customer comes in, I don't know anything."

He wiggled a finger at the stack of brochures. "You ought to know something by now."

"I mean, how to determine a correct fit, or—or—whatever."

"Let them try on some hats until they find what they like and what fits. By the time it comes to making critical decisions, I'll be back." He was already walking out. "Get you anything?"

"From the *bank*? How about several hundred-dollar bills? Or a handsome young bank guard?"

He grinned. She heard the harness brasses rattle on the door as he went out.

She heaved a sigh. This was more difficult than she had anticipated. Much. Not the work. That was easy. The difficult part was controlling her hands every time she wanted to put them on Owen. It had never been so bad before. She had always been terrifically attracted to him. Now it was almost more than anybody could be expected to bear!

Owen slammed the door on his white pickup truck

harder than necessary. He was making an idiot, not to mention a liar, of himself. Those trips into the back room to point something out to her, to ask a question—they were only to be near her. He had flanged the brim of a hat that wasn't even ready for it yet—and the other applicants had *not* been pitiful, they'd been great. He didn't need change, either. He just needed some cold, fresh air.

He wanted Sara. Surprise, surprise, and he might as well admit it—though it must make him a dirty old man—he had wanted her years ago when she was barely past being a child. He had thought the distance between them had quenched that particular fire. Now, in spite of the fact that she had grown up—he liked to think that, at thirty-one, he had, too—the fire was back.

Sara had never been a beauty, but her simple, country kind of prettiness appealed to him. It appealed to him so strongly that when he'd been near her in the back room, he had actually thought about burying his face in her hair. She curved in all the right places. She smelled like carnations, and her skin looked like a petal of the world's softest rose.

Unfortunately, the rose had thorns. Less than half a day, and already he was debating whether to corner her in the back room and kiss her until she howled, or quietly, neatly strangle her. This was going to work only if they could find some middle ground. When, he asked himself in wonder, had he ever cared about finding middle ground? Not since his grandfather's day when being allowed to stay and learn the old man's trade had frequently made him choke down his fury and pride or be banished. They had worked things out. He and Sara could work something out, too.

Thing was, he had worked things out with his grandfather because, ornery as the old man had been, Owen had basically, even if admitting it choked him, loved him. He did not have that advantage with Sara.

Gravel flew from the truck's back tires as he pulled out onto the wide highway and drove down past the campy A-frame chamber of commerce office in Payson's center. He couldn't have told, later, what he had seen or heard as he drove. His body was on automatic pilot while his mind was back in the shop, making slow, sweet, delicious love to little Sara Dugan.

THREE

The next morning, Sara finished the correspondence, stuffed the envelopes, and took them to the front counter by nine o'clock.

Owen sat on the tall stool beside the steam pot, giving a hat its final shaping, steaming its crown for a few seconds, gently tapping it with the side of his hand or giving it a delicate pinch with his fingers to form the crease, holding it off to look at it, and repeating the process. Sara watched him for a few moments, fascinated not only by the procedure, but also by his patient, delicate touch. It was only interesting, at first. Then it became rather mesmerizing, and she couldn't help imagining her own skin substituted for the felt, eased and caressed by his hands. . . .

Her face warmed when she realized he was watching her. He said, "Something I can do for you?"

She jerked herself back into reality and patted the envelopes. "These are ready. Shall I mail them?"

"Drop them on your way home, if you don't mind."

"Sure."

"Might as well get the mail and some stamps, while you're at it. Take some cash out of the drawer now, so you don't forget—and don't tell me I should write a check for something like that. Checks cost money.''

"I wasn't going to," she defended, going behind the front counter for the first time. "Do I fill out some kind of voucher?''

"Yes.''

Since he didn't add details and acted as though she was disturbing his concentration, she took a sheet from the phone pad and wrote "$10.15, Stamps," then initialed it and stuck it in the drawer. She turned to ask if there were other errands she could run, and gasped.

"Owen!"

In the glass of the big cherry-framed mirror in the corner, she could see the reflection of the mirror across the room, and reflected in *that* she could see the third mirror, the one that had always seemed to hang slightly crooked on the wall.

"Owen Dixon! You can see into the entrance!''

"What do you mean?" he inquired blandly.

She took an experimental step forward, looking, checking from different angles. She finally tore her gaze free of the reflected reflections and turned accusing eyes on him. "You can see right into the entryway from almost anywhere behind this counter!''

His eyes laughed at her. "Being the owner of this place went to my head, I guess," he said. "I thought I was *allowed* to see into the tunnel. Silly me.''

"Not only that," she added, looking at the mirror again and moving over to the wheel where he had been so busy the morning she had come to ask for the job, "you can see anybody standing at the—'' She broke off, blushing furiously while his teeth flashed in a vile grin.

"At the counter, little Sara? That what you were gonna say? You mean, like, if a girl was to sneak up behind me while I was working and do something—

let's say something mature like stick her tongue out at my back—I'd be able to see her?''

She lifted her chin and forced her eyes to meet his with as much dignity as possible. ''I owe you more than a stuck-out tongue for all the things you've done to me over the last—'' She had to stop and do some quick calculations. She had actually met him first when she was eleven years old; he had stolen the red ribbons from her braids and tied them onto the handlebars of his chopped Harley. ''Twelve years!'' she finished. ''And, if we are talking about *maturity*, I want my ribbons back, Owen!''

She turned and marched stiffly into the back room to fling herself into old Benjamin's swivel chair, writhing with embarrassment.

Owen put his elbows on the workbench, rested his head on his hands, and quietly howled with laughter.

They worked in their separate rooms for more than an hour.

Owen had chuckled for fifteen minutes, remembering the look on Sara's face and the sudden fierceness in her soft voice. She occasionally told him off, in her quiet way, but he had seldom seen such outrage in her eyes or on her face. It had made his whole day.

He was finishing the hat's braided leather band when he finally heard his grandfather's chair creak and knew Sara still lived. A chuckle almost slipped out. He quashed it. It wasn't fair to prod her. She was, after all, right, as usual. He did deserve a lot more than a stuck-out tongue.

He heard a thump, then Sara said his name in a tone he hadn't heard since his grandmother had died.

She came out scowling, with the general ledger open across her arms. He had the urge to laugh again, and then wondered at the unusual number of times he'd had that urge the last couple of days.

She plunked the ledger onto the workbench. "This is driving me crazy."

"What?"

"Your nines look like fours."

It was true, so he felt minimally guilty. "Sorry."

She was still irritated with him over the mirrors, which for some reason tickled him. "Your fours look like sevens."

"No, they don't."

"Yes, they do, and your sevens look like nines, with that stupid loop on the front of them!"

"They do not!"

"Yes, they do! Half the time, your twos look like fives, and vice versa. The only way I can know for sure is to total all the figures and see if I can tell from the total what the numbers should be!"

He reached out, pulled the ledger nearer, and gave it a quick examination. "Everything—"

The phone rang, and while he slanted a laughing look at Sara, he answered it.

Sara was still so irked she didn't even pretend not to eavesdrop when she realized the call was not a business one. It wasn't hard to tell.

"Well, he*llo*, you sweet thing," Owen murmured into the receiver. "Where in the world are you?" Then, "Is that a fact? How long will you be in town?" He swiveled two gleaming, granite eyes around to Sara, and suddenly one of them closed in a quick wink that made her feel like doing something childish again.

"You bet," he was saying. "Wouldn't miss it. You still got that shiny silver number you wore last time? Mmm, that sounds even better, darlin'. How 'bout I pick you up about seven? We'll go for steaks, then after that—we'll play it by ear. Or hand. Or mouth."

This was followed by a chuckle that was, at best, lecherous. Owen listened for a moment, his eyebrows climbing slightly in surprise—or perhaps lustful interest, Sara wasn't sure which—then murmured, "Oh, honey, you know I do. You be ready at seven, 'cause I'll be there, hotter'n a pistol."

He hung up. He looked at the phone for a moment, then, shaking his head slightly, said, "Mm-mm-*mm*!" as if he were already looking at a big, juicy steak— except Sara didn't think he was imagining food at all.

She said, "About these numbers."

Smiling, Owen looked up and handed the ledger back to her. "Little Sara, everything looks fine to me. I get sloppy sometimes. You'll cope." He glanced at his watch. "I've got to pick up a shirt. Something in silk, if I can find such an animal in this hamlet. There's just time to do it before you leave for the day."

He stood, patting his hip pocket as if checking for his wallet. "Give me those envelopes. I'll mail them." He grinned. "It's a treat, having someone to look after things. Where's that ten bucks you took for stamps?"

She took the money from the pocket of her jeans. "It's for stamps," she reminded him.

He radiated innocence. "I know it."

"I mean, it's not for steaks. Or shirts."

He actually had the gall to look wounded. "I know what it's for. I'll be back shortly."

He was whistling when he went out.

Sara watched in the mirror until he disappeared behind the door. He had stood right there, that first morning, watching her dawdle and chew her knuckles while she pondered how to approach him, watching her make an infantile face at his back and said never a word. No wonder he'd been so sarcastic with her right off the bat.

She wondered who had been on the phone. Some former girlfriend, with a slinky silver dress and the body to put in it. . . .

Sara slammed the ledger shut. The man wouldn't pay her more than minimum wage, but he could afford to buy a silk shirt. He hired extra help so his work would get caught up, then took off in the middle of the day to buy a shirt. It was irresponsible, unprofessional, delinquent behavior, and exactly what she should have expected from Devil Dixon. She dragged herself back to the pigeonhole desk. She should have asked Owen to bring her a soft drink to cleanse the sudden, crummy taste in her mouth.

In his truck, Owen was still whistling.

The girl on the phone was named Danielle. Danielle was an armful from his fairly distant past, but even though he'd arranged to pass an evening with her, he felt absolutely no stir of genuine interest. If Sara hadn't been there, he'd have made some excuse to Danielle, gone running, then put a mystery in the VCR and flopped in front of it with a bowl of chili.

His behavior was a little silly, admittedly, but he just couldn't resist. Maybe he'd never be able to stop playing little jokes on Sara, no matter how old he got. The look in her eyes as she listened to him make the date had been priceless. Shock, at first. After he winked at her, disgust. Then, indignation. Sara was always good at indignation.

He switched tunes, whistling something trickier as he pulled into the center where the town's only Western-wear store was located. He did need a new shirt, but he detested silk.

Working with Sara was more interesting than TV, Owen thought cheerfully. She was jealous as all get-out.

Next morning, Owen looked as if he'd overslept and hadn't had time to shave, or maybe he'd spent the night somewhere away from his razor. After Sara said "Good morning" to him and examined his face, she simply sniffed and went to what she was already thinking of as "her" desk. She didn't see his eyes gleam as he watched her go.

He left her alone until nearly ten. Then he lounged into the back room and propped himself up against the end of the desk, looking down at the journals spread around her.

"How's it going?"

"Fine," she said stiffly. "You weren't terribly far behind."

"Think you'll have time to get everything ready for Maddox?"

"Plenty. You'd better start thinking up other things for me to do. Or maybe I should just quit when I'm through here. That might make more sense. You won't actually need me after a few days."

The oddest thing happened in Owen's chest when she said that. Not need her? She had no idea what she was saying.

Sara sounded sulky. Part of him was secretly amused by that. He hadn't shaved because he had known she would think he had caroused all night with Danielle. In that sense, she had run true to form.

She hadn't reacted quite as expected, though. He'd braced to be quietly bawled out for his riotous living and sinful ways. Instead, she showed signs of retreating, and now this talk about terminating her employment. His heart banged around in his chest and a sudden light dawned. He wouldn't tolerate another four years away from Sara. Maybe he was just getting old. Sara was one of the few friends he had, something not to be sneezed at. The last time she'd left, he hadn't even known about it until she was gone. He'd had nothing to say about it. This time, he did.

Sara's emotions confused her. She felt unreasonably hurt, neglected, and let down, and she didn't know why. Owen didn't owe her any allegiance. They were only friends; at the moment, they were just employer and employee, if anything. Maybe he hadn't changed. Maybe all the things people had said about him for years were true. Maybe what she had always thought to be frustration coming out in rebellious behavior and small, cruel jokes was a truly sadistic sense of humor. Maybe he was unfeeling and selfish, arrogant and mercenary, indeed.

She returned his narrowed gaze with a calm she didn't feel. After a moment, he said, "There'll be plenty to do. Take a break now and fetch a black hat body from the stock."

She watched him walk back out through the doorway into the shop. He was wearing a dark red shirt with a black Western yoke that molded to his broad, muscular shoulders. His body didn't look ravaged or tired, but trim and powerful. He ran four or five miles a day, had since his rodeoing days. He appeared fit and healthy. If he had lived the dissipated sort of youth so many people credited to him, it certainly didn't show. He was strong; she had reason to know that. Faintly uncomfortable with that memory, she went to the cedar cupboard, chose a body, and followed him.

A customer browsed while Owen reshaped his hat for him. Sara watched Owen's hands deftly manipulate the felt until the cowboy was satisfied with the rakish dip in the brim. She listened while they discussed rope horses. When the man was about to leave, he touched the brim of his newly remodeled hat, nodded to Sara, and murmured a polite "Miss" before he walked away.

Sara found Owen's entertained eyes on her and said, "If I were a feminist, I'd hate that."

"But you didn't, did you? I almost expected to see you drop a curtsy, you looked so thrilled."

"I wasn't *thrilled*. I know it's outdated. I don't think that because a man shows a woman a little special respect it means he thinks she can't stand on her own

two legs or think for herself." She shrugged. "I like
it. It makes me feel good. How bad can it be?"

"What a good hippie you would've made!" He put
on a comically diabolical expression, hunched one
shoulder, and lowered his voice to a maniacal croak.
"Come, do lick up a little LSD, my dear. . . ."

She laughed. "You can hardly equate taking drugs
with old-fashioned manners, Owen! You're so funny."

A sudden, arrested look came into his eyes. Was that
what she thought? Funny old Owen . . . not a serious
cell in his brain.

She said, "He was the real thing, wasn't he?"

"Who? What?"

"That man. He was a real cowboy, wasn't he, not—
what do you call it? Drugstore."

"Oh. Yes. He ranches over near Haddon's. Raises
Herefords."

"I like men like that. He looked—you know, all the
Old West stuff. Hard-working, settled, and self-reliant.
He was handsome, too, in that hat."

Owen turned away slightly, suddenly angry. It
sounded as though she didn't think he fit into that cate-
gory. *Shiftless*, she probably would have said, *unstable,
and conceited, that's you*. If she thought that, nobody
was to blame but Owen Dixon. He had the odd image
of himself as one of those movie gunfighters who
couldn't hang up his guns because his reputation pur-
sued him wherever he went. He swallowed the surge
of emotion and reached to take the hat body from her.

"Let me show you how this whole process starts."

Her lovely, big eyes were startled at first, then he
saw the stirring of hope deep in them.

"Have you changed your mind? Are you going to
teach me?"

There were a hundred things he'd like to teach her,
most of which had nothing to do with hatting. *We'll
start with kissing, I think. How much practice have you*

had? How good a kisser are you, little Sara? A small flash fire swept through his body when he thought about it, and his hands were suddenly not quite steady on the black felt.

"No," he said firmly. "I'm showing you the process, so you can talk to customers about it. I don't expect you to remember everything, but you'll have a better idea of what I do and why I ask them to allow me two months to do it."

She looked so disappointed that he wanted to take her in his arms. *Brother, you are deranged.*

He picked up a heavy chunk of maple. He didn't look at Sara's face, afraid that, if he did, he would see such sadness or pleading in her eyes that he'd become a complete idiot, agreeing to teach her anything she wanted to know, just to keep her with him as long as possible.

"This is a block. First step—I put the body on it, then put it upside down in the steam pot to form the crown."

Sara had no idea why Owen was acting oddly, but he was showing her more than he had agreed to, a move in the right direction. She watched as his proficient hands worked through each step. When he reached a point where the hat required standing time in order to dry out and set its shape, he had another hat already in progress to illustrate the next stage. She followed everything closely, occasionally asking for clarification.

When the hat was blocked and the crown height set with a blocking cord, the hat went on the wheel to be pounced.

"This is pouncing paper."

"I know that. It looks like sandpaper."

"That's what it is, basically. I start with coarse and work down to very fine, until the felt has a smooth finish. Try it. Easy. Always clockwise."

"Why?"

"Because of the way the fur's applied to the cone by the felter."

"If this is sandpaper, why don't you call it sandpaper?"

"Because it's pouncing, not sanding."

"Why is it called pouncing?"

"It's an old term . . . something like . . ." He searched his memory for an ancient lesson. "I think, instead of sand, they originally used a powder made out of bone—like pumice. The word *pounce* comes from some French word. Stop asking logical questions."

A customer interrupted them. The elderly man was uncertain about "these newfangled styles." Owen patiently worked with him until the man found a comfortable style, and determined the size, color, and quality, based on the man's needs and wallet. Sara hovered as Owen wrote up the order, and the specifications she'd seen on the cards in the file box began making sense. Owen's manner was friendly and businesslike, shaming Sara for her earlier thoughts about him.

When the customer departed, they returned to the hat. Owen luhred the crown, using a soft cloth and luhring grease.

"It's some kind of petroleum product. It helps replace the natural oils in the fur. Makes it more weatherproof and gives it a sheen."

"It should be called 'alluring' grease. Get it? Luhring—alluring?"

"You're a scream."

A brass sizing ring went into the hat to steady it while the brim was flanged. Then the brass ring was changed to a maple one, and the brim was pounced and luhred.

"This particular customer likes a soft hat, so I'll finish with a touch of spray sizing. If he wanted a stiffer hat, or one particularly waterproof, I'd use more."

"It's like ironing."

"Gee, ironing—honey, you're more domestic than I'd dreamed."

"I know what ironing is. I didn't say I actually do it."

The brim was trimmed to the ordered width, the edge carefully sanded smooth and symmetrical. The sizing ring was changed again, and the hat went into the flanging bag, a big sandbag with a heating coil in it. The weight of the sand combined with heat would press the brim flat and even.

The sweatband was stamped with the customer's name, Owen's name, and the appropriate number of X's, then it and the lining were sewn into the hat.

"Now," Owen said with satisfaction as he picked up a hat that was all but finished, "I give her a little steam, a little shaping—keep the steam *light*, I can't say that enough—a little more shaping—then I let her dry thoroughly, add the band, and she's ready to go."

Although she'd done nothing but some pouncing, and had never lain a finger on the particular hat Owen held, Sara also felt a certain satisfaction. She flicked the brim with her forefinger. "Crisp, thin, like velvet. Am I getting the right idea, boss?" She grinned at him and found him watching her with a peculiarly intense look that wiped the smile off her face. His eyes snagged hers. Her hand, poised next to his, felt the warm draw of his skin. "I—" Her mouth was dry. She tried again, "I want—to learn, more than ever, Owen."

His eyes watched her, unwavering and darkening, drawing her toward him. Before she could pull away, he put out a hand and tucked her hair behind her ear.

"You have pretty little ears." His voice was quiet, huskier than usual. He tipped his head forward, his mouth hovering just above hers. She felt the warmth of his breath on her lips. He smiled suddenly, a warm and gentle smile she had never seen before. Never. She felt its touch in her middle, as surely as if he had put his hand on her belly. "Shame to cover them up, even with this beautiful, silky honey."

He put the hat on one of the long, curved brass hooks above the workbench and looked away, releasing her eyes, with the smile still lingering on his lips. "Let's get Maddox out of the way first. Then we'll talk about what I'll teach you."

Could she take that at face value or, coming on the heels of that *strange* moment between them, did it mean something else? Eventually, still stupid with surprise, she managed to say, "Thanks—for showing me what you have."

There could be a double meaning there, too. Thanks for showing me a new smile, a new gentleness? She herself didn't know what she meant. This was confusing, but exciting, too. Owen made her feel things she had never felt before. She had always been attracted to him, but this was something entirely new and . . . out of the question. Robert would have a fit. Besides, her heart had been bruised too recently. She did not need the additional pain of loving a man like Owen. Almost anybody she knew would say it was stupid. Absolutely out of the question.

But when Owen said, "Let's walk over to Aunt Ada's for lunch. I'll spring," her heart leaped up like a house dog ready for walkies.

She did try to resist. "I planned to have a sandwich when I got home."

Owen smiled again, the old smile with the faintly wolfish teasing in it. "Suit yourself. It's the only perk you get with this job. Don't seem smart to pass it by."

"True." She brightened. It wasn't as though he was asking for a date. It was lunch with the boss. Perfectly legitimate business activity, even tax deductible. "That'd be a nice change from my own cooking. When? . . ."

"Now."

She looked at her watch and was shocked. "Good grief, it's nearly two."

"Come in late tomorrow if it bothers you, but I don't object to paying for extra time. You were working."

"It didn't feel like working. I hope you'll change your mind."

"Sara . . ."

"Okay—we're waiting until the Maddox business is settled, but whatever, I still want to learn to do a hat from beginning to end. That would make me feel so good!"

"You're weird. Get your purse."

"But what do we do about the shop?"

"What do you think I did before I hired you, listen to my empty stomach growl? We lock the door and put up the 'Gone to Lunch' sign. Get your purse. Your jacket, too. The breeze is kicking up."

He was being gruff and pushy, but she didn't mind. She walked beside him across the small graveled parking lot, down the drive, toward the highway. Owen didn't hurry. He put his hands into the pockets of his handsome red-and-gold blanket coat, against the chilly breeze, and walked slowly through the shafts of sun slanting through the ponderosa pines.

Halfway down the drive, he pulled one hand from a pocket long enough to indicate a path through the trees, and they turned off into the woods.

"Looks like you come this way often."

"I eat at Aunt Ada's a couple times a week. This beats walking along the highway."

There was silence between them for a few minutes. He had been right about the breeze. In spite of the bright sunshine, the temperature was below fifty degrees. Sara zipped up her jacket and put her hands into the pockets, unconsciously mimicking Owen.

"It's chilly. I'm glad you made me bring my jacket."

"I'm not right as often as you are; I hit it once in a while."

She looked at him askance. "What is *that* supposed to mean?"

"Haven't you noticed?" He flashed her an ironic look. "You're right all the time."

That was ludicrous. She said so.

"Let's talk about something else, then. How about: Where's your engagement ring?"

Her eyes flew to his, then veered off. "What are you talking about?"

"Robert told me you'd gotten engaged. I don't see a ring on your finger."

"My big-mouthed brother neglected to tell you I'm un-engaged. Not that it's any of your business."

" 'Course not. Must be near two years ago he told me. What happened?"

"I thought we just agreed it's none of your business."

"We did. What happened, little Sara?"

The second time he asked, his voice was surprisingly gentle. Sara flipped through the various excuses she had dispensed for the last year and a half, all true, in their way. *We decided we weren't compatible. We came to realize we had different priorities. Things simply didn't work out.* Nice, clean little excuses.

She looked at Owen again. As they walked along, his gray eyes often moved to her. If she didn't answer, he would pursue it until he got an answer, and if she gave him one of her excuses, he'd recognize it as one.

She took a deep breath and spoke the plain truth aloud for the first time. "I was dumped."

He laughed.

Sometimes he could cut her to the bone and not even notice. "It's not funny."

"I'm laughing with you, not at you."

"But I'm not laughing."

He modified the laughter into a grin. "It's just the

way you said it. You'd think it had never happened before.''

"It never happened to *me* before," she said ruefully. "I suppose you've dumped so many women you don't think of it as a big deal.''

His grin disappeared, replaced by a scowl. "Thanks. You have a nice opinion of me. I've never dumped a woman.''

She turned wide eyes on him. "What about the string of girls you've had over the years? Are you saying they just sort of—what—beamed up?''

"Yes. No. Maybe it's a question of meaning. To me, being 'dumped' isn't the same as agreeing a relationship won't develop or work out. I'm not the kind of jerk who gets deeply involved with a woman then dumps her.'' His conscience prickled faintly. "It irks the heck out of me that you don't have anything better to do than listen to gossip.''

"Well, if you spend your life building up a reputation, you shouldn't be surprised if people base their judgment of you on it.''

There it was again, his reputation following him around like a devoted dog. If Sara believed all the diverse escapades credited to him over the years, why had she stuck by him?

They crunched along in the pine needles for a bit. "You believe all that trash about me, do you?''

"No . . . I believe half of it.''

"Not even half is true.''

Sara looked at him closely. This was interesting and novel: Owen was concerned about what somebody thought of him. He wasn't putting it on, either; wasn't joking. He was genuinely incensed by his so-called bad reputation. Why should he be upset because she seemed to think he was as much of a reprobate as everyone else did?

She said, "You mean like Bob Bonham's Big Birthday Bash?"

"Just a quiet little party."

"I was there."

He looked startled. She added, "Robert took me. You got up in front of all those people and sang three extremely pornographic verses of 'Sweet Betsy From Pike.' "

His grin was mildly rueful. "By special request."

"From?"

"From Bob Bonham. He taught me the song. It was his birthday. I couldn't insult the man by refusing to sing it. Besides, it broke up the entire crowd."

"It was disgusting."

"You had no business being there. It was an adult party."

"That's funny, it seemed pretty juvenile to me."

He shrugged it away.

"What about the knife fight? I don't remember who it was with. It was on the street, in front of that tatty old bar that burned down six or eight years ago."

"The Goodnuff," he said with a mild sneer. "It was in the parking lot, and it wasn't a knife fight."

"The paper said you had knives."

"We had knives on us. We weren't using them. It was a fist fight, and we both walked away from it."

"I get it. Any fight you can walk away from is a good one."

"Kid's stuff."

"Ah. Would that also explain the following summer you spent riding with that motorcycle gang?"

His black brows drew together in a frown. "You know all about that, do you?"

"Everybody did."

"Were you there?"

"What?"

"Were you there? Did you ride with me that sum-

mer? Did you see me spend a summer with a motorcycle gang?"

"No, of course not, but everybody—"

"Everybody be damned!" he said softly, so savagely
that she flinched. The muscles beneath his darkly shadowed jaw were working. He was, she realized, very
angry. At her? At ignorance and low-minded gossip?
At himself?

She asked softly, "You didn't spend a summer
with—them?"

"Give the lady a cigar."

"Well, Owen, why didn't you ever *say* so?"

"Because it's never been anybody's business! If I
wanted to spend a summer standing on my head in four
feet of banana pudding, it's nobody's business!"

"What did you do that summer, then? I remember
when you came home." Even as she said it, she realized how odd the memory seemed when compared to
the man beside her, with his neat, conservative haircut
and his boots and wide hat. "You had a *ponytail,* and
a *beard,* and you looked like you hadn't had a bath
since the Vietnam War."

He shot a swift glance at her, a gleam in his gray
eyes. "Yeah? My chopper's stolen red ribbons were all
tattered, too."

Since this was a reminder of yesterday's excuse for
having stuck her tongue out at his back, she felt color
rise into her cheeks. "What did you do that summer?"

He sighed and slowed his pace so that they were
barely moving. "I rode out with the gang because I
knew my grandfather would hear about it and hate it
with all his heart. I stayed with them for three days,
but I couldn't take it. Too much drugs and scuz for
me. What?" He asked, at her expression.

"I didn't know there could be too much drugs and
scuz for you."

"Well, *thanks* again. Contrary to popular belief, I

never robbed any old ladies, I don't think sex is an Olympic sport, and I never did drugs—my one and only puff on a joint made me heave my guts all over the shoes of the guy who gave it to me. I did not do drugs.''

"Guess you don't consider alcohol a drug, then?"

He shot a hard look at her. "It's a doggone shame I wasn't allergic to alcohol, too."

"Yes," Sara agreed with a pleasantness she did not feel. They had come to a part of Owen that had always scared her.

"I know what you're thinking. I'm the first to admit I always was too quick to jump into a can or a bottle when things got rough. Then there came that one year. . . . It was a bad year." It had been such a bad year that he couldn't remember much of it, though he preferred not to admit that. He spoke quietly. "I dried out and got on with my life. No matter what people think now, I don't drink anymore. Period. That's the truth."

She glanced at him, but he was looking off into the pines. Sheer God's miracle had saved him during that bad time, she knew. He had kept away everyone who wanted to help him, his grandfather, Haddon, even her. The heavy drinking had begun right after Halloween, and she had always wondered if there was any connection. Her ego wasn't large enough to imagine that her rejection of him that night had been enough to drive him to drink, but she knew something desperate had driven him that night. She had assumed that the same desperate something had driven him right on into drinking. He had been seeing a girl regularly then. It had seemed to be serious, but they had broken up that fall.

Unconsciously, she moved closer to him as they walked. "What made you stop?"

For a moment she thought he wasn't going to answer. Then he said evenly, "Boredom, mostly."

She wasn't sure that was more than a flip answer, but she accepted it. Owen had always liked action, the outdoors, fun. Being drunk nine-tenths of the time was bound to put a damper on things. "You took yourself by the scruff of the neck and shook some sense into yourself."

The metaphor seemed to interest him. His eyes flashed over to her with an amused glint in them.

"I was proud of you for that," she said.

She wished she had told him so years sooner. He jerked his gaze away, but not before she had seen the amusement vanish. The trees suddenly seemed to fascinate him. His throat worked in a hard swallow.

She felt her heart beginning to soften up to the point of near uselessness. In cruel defense, she asked, "What about Melanie Page?"

He turned on her, his eyes icy cold. He yanked one hand from its pocket and pointed a finger at her like a gun. His voice was soft and lethal.

"We are not gonna talk about Mel Page!"

A shiver of fear scampered down her spine. *"Sorry."*

He shoved the hand back in its pocket, his stance arrogant and threatening. He looked at her for a long moment, then, in the same harsh voice, said, "I'll say this, and it's all I'm gonna say: Mel Page's baby was not mine."

She knew the flat, emotionless tone of his voice was exactly opposite of what he felt. Flooded with compassion for him, she narrowly avoided saying the wrong thing.

"I never thought it was."

He gave a derisive snort. "Then you're the only person in Payson who didn't."

"Haddon—" She stopped. Again, she had almost let out something she wasn't even supposed to know about. Owen didn't notice. "I would have married her if it had been mine. I would have taken care of them." Still flat. Still emotionless.

"I know," she said gently. "But you did sleep with her."

"Oh, did I?"

She gave a small shrug. "One day, that fall, Robert and I went up to hike from Zane Gray's cabin. Robert always drove out that way, past Mel's house. It was early in the morning, barely light. I saw you coming out of her house."

"Circumstantial evidence." His eyes came back to her, sharp and hard. "I never claimed to be a monk."

She didn't know why she'd brought this up. The whole subject and his reaction to it was making her miserable. Searching for a way out of it, she asked, "What about the Model T?"

He gave a sudden, relieved cough of laughter, as if grateful for the release of tension. "You little wretch. How long does this litany of my sins go on?"

She grinned. "I dunno. I don't want to skip anything interesting. What about the Model T?"

He had all but forgotten that escapade. On a bet, he had sneaked into the garage where a retired college professor stored his prized, restored Model T Ford, and, in one fascinating night, disassembled it and hid the parts all over town. He had kept out of jail only by reassembling the car to the owner's and the sheriff's satisfaction.

He shook his head. Most of the things she had paraded out seemed to upset her more than they did him. Some of them might be bad enough; she didn't even know the real hair curlers. He hoped she never would.

"That really was kid's stuff, and way before your time," he finally said with a gradually fading smile. "You can't hold anything before your time against me. People change."

"That was then, this is now?"

"That's right," he said firmly. "You've been away, girl. Four years. A man can change in four years."

"Of course he can," she agreed with deceptive gentleness. "That would explain why, winter before last, you rode down the middle of the Beeline Highway on a horse stark naked."

"That horse had hair all over him!"

She laughed. "You know what I mean."

He shook his head, with several *tsks* of his tongue. "Sara, Sara, Sara. When will you learn not to listen to gossip?"

"It's not gossip! Robert was there. He saw you!"

"He didn't saw me very close. If he had, he—and everybody else—would have known I was wearing beige trunks. And, I'll tell you something everybody seems to have conveniently forgotten. That was *for charity*!"

"Sure, Owen."

"Sara! The regulars at Mario's put three hundred dollars in a kitty and said if I did that stunt they'd contribute it to the American Heart Association drive the ladies' club was having. It *snowed* that day. It's a wonder I didn't need the American Heart Association myself by the time I was through.

"I'll tell you something else, young lady. I asked Haddon to bring me up a smooth-backed horse, and he brought up one with a spine like a scalpel. 'Oh,' he says to me with that deadpan face of his, 'I thought you said you wanted a smooth-*mouthed* horse'! I come real close to having to change my name to Mary Lou."

Sara was giggling when he finished. Looking at each other, laughing, they popped out of the trees directly across from Aunt Ada's Café, where a narrow side road joined the Beeline. Sara was giggling so hard she didn't even see the car cutting a tight right-hand turn into the side road, headed straight for her.

FOUR

Afterward, Sara regretted not even having had the chance to let out a decent terrified scream. Owen's hands clamped painfully on her arm and shoulder, yanking her out of the way. She spun around, emitted an unrefined squawk, and came to rest with her nose squashed against Owen's chest, her hands scrabbling at the woolly cloth of his coat.

"You blind, stupid fathead!" Owen roared after the car. The driver probably didn't hear a word, and it didn't do Sara's hearing any good, but it undoubtedly made Owen feel better, so she forgave him. His arms encircled her protectively, strong and hard. She turned her face to free her nose and discovered that, with her cheek pressed between the halves of his open jacket, she could feel his heart thudding like thunder in his chest. Aside from the fact that her knees were beginning to quiver in reaction, and there didn't seem to be enough air in the world, this felt good. She laced her fingers together behind him and held on.

Then it got more confusing. One of Owen's hands lifted and stroked her hair. His lips nuzzled her ear; the whiskers on his unshaven chin scraped her skin and sent a delicious shiver through her. His sandy voice demanded softly, "Are you all right, precious?"

Precious.

It meant nothing. He'd always flung endearments at women. Sweetheart. Honey. Darlin'. Whatever he thought would make them feel good. The better a woman felt, after all, the more likely he was to score. But *precious* was a new one, and the way he said it was new, too. She was sure of it. Or maybe she was just momentarily witless. . . .

She squirmed to free herself from his arms. "I'm fine," she gasped. "It just scared me half to death. Where did he come from?"

"He was really movin'. I don't want to wish anybody bad luck, but I genuinely hope a big, sturdy tree jumps out in front of him shortly."

"Owen!" She squirmed again. It wasn't working. All she was accomplishing was to make herself ever more aware of him as a man. His chest was hard and unyielding against her breasts. His arms were clamped around her like steel, while that one big hand stroked her hair so gently. That hand, she noticed suddenly, trembled slightly. "Owen, I can't breathe!"

The feeling was mutual. Only the people in cars whizzing by on the Beeline could see the dazed look on Owen's face. It was partly caused by nearly seeing Sara mashed before his eyes, but it was mostly caused by the wildfire that had started in him for the second time that day. Hadn't anybody ever told Sara what could happen to a man when a woman slid and wriggled up against him like that? His body had gone rigid with a sudden, hot, demanding desire he hadn't felt in a long time. If that wasn't enough, she smelled good, like a combination of clean, feminine skin and light, sweet shampoo, the kind of smell a man wanted to bury himself in when he rolled over in bed in the morning. This was *Sara*! Certain things were not permissible in the world. Thinking thoughts like this about Sara was one of them.

"Owen—I can't breathe!"

He realized she had said that at least once, and he had just stood like a big, smoldering log, feeling her honeyed silk hair under his fingers.

"Along the highway in plain sight, this way," he said unsteadily, "be a wonder if someone who knows us doesn't see us. The grapevine will have us engaged, married, and with five kids before nightfall." He loosened his grip and, holding her by the shoulders, eased her away and looked down into her face. "Sure you're all right?"

"Outside of my knees feeling like jelly, you mean? Yes."

"Let's go someplace we can sit down. My knees don't feel too trusty right now, either."

He clamped one hand around one of hers while they dashed across the busy Beeline to the café. Inside, they hung their jackets and Owen's hat on the rack by the door. They sat across from each other in a booth in the back, where the window looked out on a miniature conifer garden, sharing the unspoken opinion that they had seen all they wanted to of the highway for the moment.

When the waitress, fifty and too plump for her blue uniform, brought menus, Owen winked at her and said, "Hello, Sheila m'love. What's good today?"

Sheila pursed her orange mouth. "You are—if you're any judge."

"Well, one for Sheila. What's the special?"

"It's on the blackboard. If you could read, you'd know. Chicken noodle soup, reuben sandwich, and cherry pie."

Owen said promptly, "Pass."

Sheila rumbled away and Owen and Sara opened their menus. Sara looked at hers blindly, still slightly

shaken, as much by the warmth that had flowed through
her while Owen had held her as by the near miss. After
staring at the meaningless words for a few moments,
she looked up.

As if on cue, Owen's gray eyes lifted and met hers
across the table. His grin sprouted. He tossed the menu
to one side and said, "Whew."

Sara gave a nervous laugh. "Yeah. I guess so. Thank
you, Owen. You saved my neck, I think."

He gave a little dismissive shake of his head. "My
pleasure. It's a lovely neck." His eyes touched for a
moment on that portion of her anatomy. "Worth saving. What are you having?"

The almost tangible touch of his eyes made her voice
tight. "The special's fine."

When Sheila plunked water glasses down before
them moments later, he dutifully ordered the special
along with his own huge Ada burger and seasoned fries.
Sara gazed out at the delicate, tiny evergreens growing
among native stones, while Owen flirted with the waitress. Trifling, her father would have called it. It was
as natural to Owen as breathing. There wasn't a chance
in a thousand that the term *precious*, when it fell from
his mouth, meant he cared any more for her than for
cabbage.

When asked, she murmured she would like a cola,
and Sheila went away.

"Now." Owen pushed his napkin and flatware aside
and took a sip of water. "Where were we when that
psychopath interrupted us?"

"I don't remember." She took a sip of water, too.
"I think we were talking about you sliding down the
razor blade of life."

He winced. "My. You have a way with words. No,
we were through with Devil Dixon's *charity* ride. You
were about to tell me why you were dumped."

"I was not. That's none of your business."

"You save a woman's life, and what do you get for your trouble?" Owen said sadly. "How soon they forget."

"Oh, please. That's not what we were talking about, and you know it."

"No, but we were about to. You thought you had me distracted by talking about me—which is, I grant, a fascinatin' subject—but, I hadn't forgotten it, and we were about to get back to it."

"There's nothing to talk about."

His eyes gleamed. "You better tell me, little Sara. Otherwise, I'll have to imagine the details."

"That's your problem."

"I've got quite an imagination."

He did, and she wouldn't put it past him to share his diabolical imaginings with someone else. They had too many shared acquaintances. She sighed.

"Owen . . ." Nothing more would come out. She looked at him helplessly.

"Okay," he said obligingly. "I'll help you. Now, what did Robert tell me this filthy dog's name was? Ogden? Mervin?"

"Kevin!" It was the first time she had felt like laughing in conjunction with Kevin's name. "His name was Kevin. He was not a 'filthy dog.' He—he had certain ideas about what he wanted, and they didn't coincide with mine. That's all."

Sheila appeared with Sara's soup and nobody said anything except "Thank you" until she had gone away.

"That's not all," Owen said quietly as Sara tried her soup. "Good?"

She nodded. It was thick and meaty, but the subject of their conversation wasn't the ideal seasoning. She had trouble swallowing.

"If that'd been all, you would've just agreed you were making a mistake and gone your separate ways. That is not being dumped."

Sara spooned soup into her mouth. She hated this subject.

"Let's see," he continued mercilessly, smearing a fingertip in some spilled ice water, "The usual scenario is something like this: Gavin—what's his name?"

She glanced up and saw mischief in his eyes. "Kevin."

"Kevin. Ol' Kevin meets another woman, falls for her, and sends you a Dear Jane letter. How'm I doin'?"

"Lousy."

"Okay. Kevin drops by unexpectedly and finds you entertaining another man who has a better name than his. Shame on you, you little conniver, you. He tells you he never wants to see you again. How'm I doin'?"

Sara concentrated on chasing a noodle that was trying to escape over the rim of the cup. It was not funny. She resented him for making her feel like laughing about it.

"Lousy."

He sighed. "Okay . . . when you sleep together, you discover he's lousy—you notice I've adopted your word—in bed. You tell him so, he's royally ticked off and dumps you. How'm I d—" He broke off. Sara's big brown eyes had finally abandoned her soup, rising suddenly to meet his—distressed—then darting away to look out the window. Pay dirt?

"So that's it."

"No!" Her voice was hushed. She swung her gaze back to her soup. "That is not it. Stop it, will you? You're embarrassing me."

He wasn't sure why it was essential to have this out in the open, but it was. He wanted to know. He wanted her to tell him. If she wouldn't, he wanted to know any way he could. "A little alteration in the scene. He discovers *you're* lousy in bed, so he dumps you."

Her spoon went down into the soup and stayed there. Her hands disappeared below the tabletop and, he knew, clenched there. Her eyes hid from his. He said softly, "Bingo."

"No," she said. He could barely hear her, but her tone was resolute. "Not bingo."

He sat in silence, watching her. The breeze had ruffled her gold bangs. She hadn't bothered fussing about them. Her cheeks were pink, maybe from the chilly breeze, but probably because he was talking about sex. For one moment, he wanted to get up and move to the other side of the booth. He had the feeling a comforting arm around her would not be unwelcome.

He didn't move. He liked to think he had developed some likeness of a conscience, some semblance of ethics. Since Sara had come to the shop to weasel a job out of him, he had honorably drawn lines where she was concerned, then a few days, or a few hours—sometimes a few seconds, for Pete's sake—later, he stepped over the line and kicked dust on it. A comforting arm was too likely to become something else too quickly.

Things between them had already gone as far as he could allow. The only outcome of going further was another "dumping" for Sara. Maybe there had been a time when he wouldn't have let that bother him, but now it would be a dirty trick he couldn't stomach. Still, as he contemplated the next scenario he was about to offer, he felt a stir of excitement that refused to be squelched.

He said, "I get one more try."

She surprised him by lifting her chin and looking at him directly. "According to what rule?"

"My rule. One more try. Marvin . . . what's his name?"

She allowed a twisted smile. "Kevin."

"Kevin took your mind off your troubles. You needed a man's support about then. Your daddy was sick. Your brother wasn't there. Kevin filled the bill. He seemed like a decent guy. You thought you loved him. You decided to marry him. Everything was hunky-dory until he wanted you to prove you loved him by . . . being intimate with him. You wouldn't. He pushed you, but you—being a stubborn young lady—wouldn't give in. He dumped you. How'm I doin'?''

She nodded miserably, silently, and stared at her soup.

"Your soup's getting cold."

"I can't eat." Her voice was small, defeated. It wrung his heart.

"Okay." He reached over, took the soup cup, and finished the soup silently. It was delicious, and he was happy, doggone it! He knew he should be woeful, for her sake. He wasn't. He'd stopped short of asking Sara if she had ever had a man, but not because he was kind. He didn't have to ask. His gut told him. It was an exciting, really choice idea—Sara grown into a lovely woman, and virtually untouched—a pointless idea, since he already had decided their relationship could go no further. It didn't even make sense to him, but he *liked* Sara better than ever.

Sara looked out the window until their sandwiches came. By then she was able to give Sheila a smile of thanks. She didn't look at Owen, but she took her knife and sliced the thick sandwich in half. She sipped her soft drink, then sat and picked escaped caraway seeds off the plate, putting them back onto the bread.

"Sara."

Slowly, her eyes came up and met his.

"It wasn't a crime," he said quite gently. "Saying no was your right and your privilege. He was a selfish jerk in my opinion, which you get whether you want it or not. Honey, that's the oldest line in the book: 'If you won't go all the way, then you don't love me.' I'm pleased to say I haven't used it since I was seventeen."

Sara chewed on her lip. It was a relief, actually, to have someone know the truth. Not even her brother knew what had actually broken Kevin and her up; Robert had thought Kevin a fine, upstanding young gentleman, in every sense of the word. . . . Well, Owen had been kinder than she had expected. A man with Owen's reputation might have sided with Kevin.

She cleared her throat. "I know. I know you're at least partially right. But I knew him for nearly two years. At least, I thought I knew him. You can't imagine how childish and—*stupid* he made me feel."

He gave her the oddest look. Impossibly, she saw pain in his eyes for a split fraction of time. "Don't be so sure."

Then the look was gone. He wiggled a french fry in the direction of her plate. "Get on the outside of that. I'm paying for it, so every crumb had better be cleaned up."

She got off to a slow start, but as they chatted about lighter subjects, she managed to eat the sandwich and some of Owen's fries—it seemed fair, since he had eaten her soup. By the time Owen paid the check and they went out into the cool afternoon, she felt halfway human again.

As they walked back up the shortcut trail, Sara said shyly, "It was nice of you not to laugh at me."

"Yeah, that's me. Kick a woman when she's down, every time."

"I didn't mean that. But you have been known to make a joke out of somebody else's trouble. I—I never told anyone why Kevin and I broke up before."

He sent her an accusing smile. "You haven't told anyone *yet*."

She sighed. "I'm sorry. I've never been able to—get the words out. I couldn't tell Dad. He was too sick. He knew he wouldn't live much longer and was happy thinking Kevin would take care of me after he died. I couldn't tell Robert. He was busy building his practice up here in Payson, and he thought Kevin was solid gold—and he can be such an overprotective blockhead. . . . Anyway, I couldn't begin to talk about *that* to Robert.''

Owen wasn't quite sure how to take that. She couldn't begin to talk about *that* to her own brother, but she could to him. Where did that put him in the scheme of things?

"No girlfriends?"

She shrugged lightly. "The girls I knew in Phoenix thought I was an idiot for letting Kevin get away. I just told them we had decided we weren't compatible. To them, anything I might have done to keep him would have been worthwhile. He had a little money, you see, or he would when he turned twenty-five. . . .''

"Why, you little gold digger, you.''

"He was also—I don't know. *Suave* sounds rather 1930-ish, but I guess that's as good a word as any. Polished and upwardly mobile. A very hard worker.''

"I hate his guts.''

"There were good things about him. Really.''

"Why didn't you sleep with him?''

She swallowed a gasp. "I told you—''

"I mean, did you not do it because you didn't think it was moral? Or did you not do it because he didn't turn you on?''

She concentrated on the toes of her shoes. If she were to look up and find him grinning, she would shrivel down like the doused wicked witch in *The Wizard of Oz*. "Both. I—guess.''

"But if you'd wanted him, if you'd gotten caught up with him in passion—you might have waived that belief that it wasn't right?''

She looked startled when he asked that. Her pink blush always delighted him.

"I don't know.'' She had to admit that passion had been somewhat truant when she was with Kevin. She said softly, "I guess that's one of those things you don't know about until it happens."

"Do you miss him?"

Good question. She hadn't thought about Kevin in a while, except to realize she had been immature and naive where he was concerned. She knew now that she hadn't needed him as much as she had thought. "I did at first. We had fun, but—I guess I don't miss him much."

"It was the right thing to do, then. . . . Is that why you moved back here?"

"Not exactly." *You're here*. She didn't dare say it. "Payson is still home. I'd never have left in the first place if the doctors hadn't said Dad needed better medical facilities after his stroke. . . . He could barely speak, you know. I was the only one who could understand him a little. We hoped he could get past that with good rehab therapy."

Owen was silent for a couple of steps. Then he said evenly, "Four years down there, though—and he died anyway. What was the point? You might as well have brought him back up here and let him die among his friends."

She darted a sharp look at him. "Why are you being cruel?"

"I'm not."

"Yes, you are! He didn't want to be with his friends! He didn't— After his second stroke, he was paralyzed, Owen. He couldn't move, he couldn't talk. Someone had to do *everything* for him. His face was twisted. He didn't want his friends to see him like that." Her voice quivered. "He didn't even want Robert to see him like that." She saw Owen's eyes turn to her, sharing her misery, making an unspoken apology for his thoughtlessness. She said more lightly, "Anyway, I never liked Phoenix. Too big and busy. Too hot in the summer. When I lost my job, I just came home."

"You're planning to stay here for good, then?"

"Depends on what kind of job I find. I hope so. I have to support myself, though."

"I'll give you a letter of reference. You can type it yourself. It may do you more harm than good, though, in this community."

"I wish you wouldn't say things like that! Give Payson a break! It's a lovely place! It's grown so that half the population never even heard of you—and there are people who admire and respect you and give you credit for the good things you've done." She cast a laughing glance at him, saying in a phony, serious little voice, "You're a member of the chamber of commerce, and you do things *for charity*."

"An hour ago you were telling me I'm a scoundrel. Now I'm a saint!"

"Not quite! . . . But it bothers me to hear you say belittling things about yourself."

He didn't reply. They came out by the shop. At the steps, Owen said, "You might as well go home. I may go early myself, if I don't have a customer." He grinned and rubbed his chin. "Hot date tonight. I don't think she'd appreciate me showin' up like this."

Hot date. Why did she have the unreasonable urge to scratch out somebody's eyes? She turned toward her car. "Same person as last night?"

"You bet."

"Then you'd better go home early and take a nap."

He gave a little chuckle. "Hey, Sara?"

She paused just inside the open car door. He came around the front of the car and looked down at her. "You don't know my brother Drew, do you?"

"I met him once years ago. Why?"

He put his hands in his coat pockets and jingled keys or change in one of them. "He's bringing his family down from Colorado for a visit. It'll be the first time I've seen him in years."

"Oh?" she said, wondering what she was expected to say about it.

"He and his family will stay at Haddon's for a while. We're supposed to get together Sunday for lunch and whatnot. Barbecue, if the weather's right. I thought maybe you'd go out there with me."

The invitation was such a surprise that she couldn't help staring. Owen looked strange as he waited for her response, as if he had surprised himself by asking.

"Owen, that's nice of you, but—I don't think it would be right. It's a family thing, and—"

He made a little motion with his chin that dismissed that. "Don't be foolish. You know Haddon; he likes you—better than he likes me, probably. He's invited a couple of people you know. Drew and I, well, we never did get along. His wife is a cool little number, and his kids—still an unknown quantity. Frankly, in a gathering like that, I could use somebody on my side. Come on, Sara. *Free food.*"

"Believe it or not, I do have other priorities!" she said crossly.

Her tone made him grin. "I thought I'd have you clean out the cupboards in the back room tomorrow. There're some things of Granddad's in there that I want out before Maddox comes. I thought we could box them up and take them out to Haddon's. There's all kinds of family stuff stored in his attic."

"That's neat. That you're saving those kinds of things, I mean. Since they'll never know your grandfather, your kids will love them someday."

The silence screamed. Owen's eyes were on her but suddenly were seeing right through her to another place or time, she wasn't sure exactly what. He came back slowly, an odd, bitter smile playing around his mouth. "Right," he agreed at last. "How about it?"

She intended to say no, but somehow, when she

opened her mouth, the words "Okay. I'd like it" came out.

"Good. Tell Robert to come, too."

"I thought you didn't like Robert. I've never heard you say a complimentary thing about him."

"I didn't want to swell his pointed little head. Ask him."

"All right, but he'll be on call this weekend."

"It's only a few miles away. He has a radio or pager or something, doesn't he?"

"Yes."

"Ask him. Tell him to bring a date. You too, if you want."

"Okay," she said uncertainly. "I'll probably just come with Robert."

He gave the car door a gentle nudge. "See you in the morning."

She said good-bye and drove away, tired but curiously relieved. They had been easier with each other than in all the years she had known him. In spite of all her shyness, she had always been able to talk to Owen, but he had never before opened up so much to her.

There were just two blots on the day. There was a slight feeling of deflation that had remained after Owen had advised her to bring a date. Until that moment, she had almost had the silly idea she was to be his date. Then there was that one little thing for which she was kicking herself. "Kids," she said aloud, "you idiot, you should never have mentioned kids!"

Owen stood on the steps, watching her go. Something terrific and terrible had happened that day. A better bond had forged between Sara and himself; that was a terrible mistake. He couldn't see himself doing anything to break that bond. He should. He wouldn't. If he could have a few sweet days . . . until Sara quit working for him, maybe. That would be time enough, all the time a man could reasonably expect to have.

Then he could turn villain again, and nobody would be particularly surprised. *Oh, that's just Dixon, sliding off into the mire again.*

He turned back to the shop, digging the key from his Levi's pocket as he climbed the steps.

"Coward."

Nobody argued with him.

FIVE

Thursday morning was so cloudy that Sara had to turn on the lamp when she sat down to work at the pigeonhole desk. Promptly, a wink of light from the cushion of old Benjamin's overstuffed chair caught her eye and she reached down into its seat.

An earring . . . a small, classy cluster of diamonds and amethysts set in white gold.

In the shop, Owen was sitting on the stool, clipping the stained lining out of a hat that was in for renovation. He looked up, saw the expression on Sara's face, and asked warily, "What did I do now? Do my eights look like twelves?"

She studied him deliberately. "I'm rather disappointed, Owen," she said musingly.

"By what?"

"I had always thought of you as more the gold-and-pearls type." Watching his face, she extended her fist and revealed the piece of jewelry.

One of his eyebrows winged up. He took the earrings from her palm and held it up to the light. "Pretty thing. I reckon Danielle must've lost it last night." He slipped the earring into the pocket of his blue plaid shirt and snapped the flap shut. "Where'd you find it?"

"In your grandfather's chair." She couldn't help it if her voice was tinged with annoyance. "The big, cozy one."

He swung eyes full of aware amusement around to her face. "It is big and cozy, isn't it? Big enough for two, if they're friends."

Friends seemed a conservative term. "How was your 'hot date' last night?"

"Sara," he said seriously, with a frown, "there are some things a man doesn't talk about."

Her smile was frosty. "Your discretion is commendable. I'll start on the cupboards now, shall I?"

"You do that little thing."

She went quietly into the back room and began tearing the cupboards apart. She *hated* Danielle's earrings, Danielle's silver dress, and, most of all, Danielle.

Sara spent most of the morning venting her loathing by reorganizing the cupboards and shelves. The contents were not in serious disarray, but some hadn't been moved in a long while. There was an accumulation of bits of paper and dust bunnies that needed to be eliminated. She dragged out the ancient tank vacuum and cleaned every nook and cranny, putting old Benjamin's legacy in boxes as she went. She answered the phone when Owen was busy with a customer. Later, while Owen was on the phone, she made her first sale. During a break, she posted the previous day's receipts, then went back to the cupboards.

Owen kept to himself all morning. Fine. She didn't need to talk to him. In fact, she didn't want to talk to him. If she talked to him, she would see that *look* in his eyes, that knowing, laughing, mocking look. Whenever her gaze happened to fall on the chair, she was assailed by the image of what Owen and Danielle might have done in the cozy chair big enough for two. Tangles and wrappings of clothes, bare, bronzed legs and backs . . . Over and over again, she slammed a mental door on the image.

At twelve, she closed the cupboard doors, got her jacket and purse, and went out into the shop.

"I'm going now," she told Owen's back. "Everything is clean. I took out whatever was obviously your grandfather's and boxed it. You should see if there's anything you want to throw out rather than store. You should also see if I missed anything."

After a moment, Owen looked up from his work, set the hat aside, and turned on the stool to face her.

"I'll do it this afternoon. Thanks."

She felt uncomfortable about the way she had sulked over Danielle and the chair, but she couldn't quite bring herself to apologize. "I'll see you tomorrow, then."

Instead of agreeing, he pinned her with his clear gray eyes for a few seconds, then made a little motion with his hand.

"Come here."

She looked at him suspiciously. He didn't look angry. She couldn't quite identify his expression. She went closer, until his knees nearly touched the front of her thighs. "What?"

Their eyes met at the same level now. In his steady, sandy voice, he said, "You're upset about something that isn't your concern."

She opened her mouth. Nothing came out. She wasn't positive she knew what he meant, but she selected the thing she currently felt most guilty about—Danielle—and assumed it was that. She had never imagined he would mention it, but it didn't surprise her; it was like him. She said, "I don't know what you're talking about."

"Don't fib to me."

"I'm not!"

"Then don't fib to yourself." His eyes pegged her

until she wanted to squirm. He opened his mouth and took a breath to say something, then obviously thought better of it. Finally, his voice gentler, he said slowly, "Sara, I know you care about me. I've never understood why, but it's always meant a lot to me."

He took hold of two of the fingers of her left hand. "I care about you, too. That's why I'm saying this—I don't need a mother, or a keeper, or a conscience. You're better off steering clear of me. You understand me?"

She looked down at their hands, his naturally darker, tawny, large, and proficient-looking, hers pale and delicate. She turned her hand enough to curl her fingers around his. His skin felt hot and rough; just touching it sent a thrill of longing through her. It would have taken the tiniest of tugs to make her go to him, into his arms, to be held, to be loved. . . . He didn't love her. He cared about her, but he didn't love her. The misery produced by that knowledge made her throat ache.

Looking up from their joined hands, she said as steadily as possible, "I just want you to be happy. I don't believe a woman like her will make you happy. A whole string of women like her won't make you happy. I just . . . want you to be happy. That's all."

His smile was suddenly so tender that it made her heartache increase tenfold. "Little Sara—you're the sweetest thing. . . ." He gave her fingers a little squeeze and let them go. "Do me a favor now."

"What?"

"Go away and let me work."

She felt as if he had picked her up and plunged her into ice water. She slipped the hand that still tingled from his touch into her pocket where the tingling might last longer. Her smile was feeble. "Okay. See you tomorrow."

He said, "Mmm-hmm," and picked up the hat

again. He never looked up until after the harness brasses on the door had stopped rattling.

That had been the hardest thing he had ever had to do, but he had done it for her sake, he thought righteously. As always, he had wanted to protect her, comfort her. The tears in her eyes—tears he was aware were genuine, not a female gimmick—had nearly made him take her into his arms. That would have been fatal. Years ago, he could have done it and gone no further. Now . . . He glanced at the hand that had held and been held by hers. It looked normal, but it felt strange, as if she were still touching him, as if another unbreakable connection had been made.

He felt a hundred years old and contemptible. Maybe someday Sara might understand why he couldn't give her what she deserved—a man who could give her a home and children and a normal life, who was faithful and whole. A man couldn't offer himself half finished, half baked, with pieces missing, no matter how much a woman loved him, *no matter how much he loved her*.

He gave himself a mental shake. *Loved her* was just a figure of speech.

On Friday morning, Bentin Maddox phoned. After talking with him briefly, Owen propped himself against the end of the pigeonhole desk and said, "He's coming sooner than I thought. Week from today. What do you think?"

She looked up from the desk. "About what?"

"About all this!" Owen said sourly, wiggling a finger at the books and statements she was working on. "Can you have this stuff ready in time?"

"Sure." She saw his skeptical look. "I told you— you weren't that far behind. You're pretty thorough in your bookkeeping, so outside of an occasional question about what's a four and what's a nine—dig, dig—I've had very few problems. It's nice, basic sole-proprietorship bookkeeping. Daddy would have done it in twenty minutes.''

His expression didn't improve. He hated everything to do with the bookkeeping. He had to do it slowly and with the greatest care to keep from screwing it up. What she had done in days would have taken him a month.

She said, "If you're so unhappy about his coming, why don't you call off the whole thing? You know you don't want to sell, anyway. It's all a waste of everybody's time, isn't it?''

"I'll know better after I've heard his offer." He glanced across the room. "The cupboards look good."

"Thanks."

"I went through things last night. There's a letter from George Phippen. Did you see it?"

No hot date last night, then. Maybe Danielle had broken a nail. . . . She frowned. "I don't remember. Who is he?"

"He was a Western artist, big-time. Good, too. He died a few years back. I remember Granddad saying he'd made a hat for Phippen. Didn't pay much attention at the time. You know how kids are. . . . I ought to frame the letter and put it up."

"It would be a waste of time if Maddox Western Stores buys the place."

"Fortunately, I would still have the walls of my house to hang it on," he said sarcastically, pushing away from the desk. "Open the catalogs to the straws so I can look through them quick-like. I need to order one for a guy down in Tucson."

"Straws?" For an instant, she pictured a plastic tube in a soft drink. "A straw hat, you mean? I didn't know you made them."

"I don't mean a straw basket, honey. I don't like working on them much. I'll make one if somebody asks real sweet and humble."

"Would you teach me how to do that?"

"How to ask sweet and humble? In a minute."

"No! How to make a straw hat."

"If you nag me about that one more time," he said, his sandy voice gone almost silky, "I'm gonna fire you."

Sara almost stuck her tongue out at his departing back, but didn't chance it, even though there were no mirrors in the back room. It had not been an idle threat; Owen was in a snit that morning. She shook her head and went back to work.

Owen was putting a hat into the flanging bag when she straightened up from the desk later and said, "There's the balance sheet. I just have to type it. I need a break from numbers. What could I do for you?"

He glanced around briefly from the workbench, an odd look in his eyes. "Take a walk," he suggested tightly.

Could have been worse, Sara reflected. Could have been "Take a hike."

"Owen, how about if I—"

"Don't pester me today, Sara," Owen said, not even turning to look at her. "I'm not in the mood."

"I wasn't going to 'pester' you. I was going to offer a constructive suggestion. I'll save it."

"Oh, go ahead," he said acidly. "I'm all ears."

"Then you must be really funny-looking without your clothes."

It was a joke. She tossed it off and turned back to the desk, deciding maybe working on the statements until quitting time was a safer idea. His mood was too peculiar.

She never heard a thing until the sound occurred right behind her. A glance over her shoulder showed her Owen, looking at her with the *oddest* expression, while his hands methodically popped apart the snaps on the front of his white Western shirt.

She swiveled around. "What are you doing?"

"You think I'm funny-looking without my clothes?" *Pop* went a snap. The cuff snaps were already undone. His voice was husky and low-pitched, sensual and menacing, all at once. "Why don't we find out?"

She gave a little laugh, knowing it was a joke, but the reckless look in his eyes was exhilarating, too. "Owen, I was just kidding!"

"Are you sure, little Sara? Many a truth is spoken in jest. How can I be sure?" There was something threatening and uncivilized about the way he turned his head slightly as he spoke, so that he was looking at her a little sideways.

Pop.

"I found out the other day that you believe a lot of peculiar things about me. I know how you like to know the truth about everything, Sara. Now, most of them, there's no way I can prove the truth to you, one way or another. This is different. I can't have you walking around thinking I'm ears all over."

Pop.

"Because, darlin', there are some parts of me that don't come anywhere near looking like ears."

She watched in fascination as his hands moved down to the last visible snap, popped it, and drew the shirt open, allowing her a partial glimpse of his chest. The dark hair scattered there wasn't curly but straight—like the raven-black hair on his head. His skin was the rich, naturally tawny hue she had noticed when their hands were close together, a smooth, inviting, silky layer over hard, contoured muscle. She stared, fascinated, at his chest until she realized his hands were pulling his shirttail out of his Levi's to get at its last snap.

"Okay, Owen," she said instantly. "I get the message. Back to work, and no more silly jokes."

"Sara, if I don't show you, you never will know for sure, will you? Just being told won't convince you. I know you better than that. Not as well as I'm going to, though.'' He grinned.

His shirt was open now, and she watched him drag it back over his shoulders as he moved nearer. The darkness of his skin and the blackness of the hair on his chest contrasted sharply with the snowy fabric. Muscles rippled enticement across his chest and shoulders with his movements. She knew from the sudden darkening glitter of his eyes that he knew the exact moment when she started wondering how those silk-clad muscles would feel beneath her palms, what sounds he would make if she buried her mouth in that pelt of hair and kissed the warm flesh.

The shirt whipped off and drifted like a ghost into old Benjamin's overstuffed chair behind him. His hands dipped down and deftly freed the trophy buckle, a relic from his rodeo days, at his waist.

''Owen?''

''Sara? Hold your horses. I'm about to get to the best part.''

His thumb popped the big copper button out of its denim home, and his fingers moved toward the tab of his zipper. Seeing the sudden, unexpected shape of his body made her go hot all over with shock and an unforeseen, unfamiliar craving.

The harness brasses rattled. Sara jerked her eyes up to meet Owen's and whispered shakily, ''A—customer!''

''Yeah,'' Owen whispered back, rather loudly, turning toward the door. ''Golly gee whiz, I sure hope it's not a lady.''

He took one step toward the shop and Sara pounced, grabbing his arm. ''Owen! You can't go out like that.''

He shook his head. ''I can't neglect a customer, little Sara. 'Sides, it may be a married woman, and she won't be too shocked, it being nothing she's never seen before.'' He brightened. ''Hey, then I'll have independent verification that what I've been telling you is true. 'Course, now that I think of it, I could get quite a bit of that, anyway.''

Sara gasped, halfway between outrage and giggling. Pulling on his naked, hairy arm was doing absolutely nothing at all toward halting him. It only sent waves of hot, prickly sensation deep down into her middle and sucked away her breath while he dragged her closer to the door. At the last second, she slipped ahead of him, put her fist into his hard, muscle-ridged stomach, and pushed with all her strength until he came to a stop and bounced back half a step. "You put your shirt on, and don't you dare," she hissed, shoving a warning fingernail into his chest, "don't you *dare* come out like that!" She spun around and marched into the shop with a ramrod down her spine.

Owen took another step back, made unsteady by silent laughter. He swung around, picked up his shirt, slipped into it against the chill of the back room, then flung himself into the old chair, slowly fastening the snaps. It hurt to sit down, but at the moment, it hurt to stand up. Six of one and half a dozen of the other.

He tipped his head back against the chair. Well, his resolve to protect Sara from himself had lasted all of twenty-two hours. *Why*, he inquired silently of the pine ceiling, *was I given the backbone of a lower invertebrate*? Destined to be an idiot. Mad as a hatter . . . If that were true, then there wasn't a thing in the world he could do about it. He'd just have to stand—or sit— and take his punishment like a man.

He recognized the customer's voice and knew the man had come to pick up a hatband that was under the counter, plainly labeled with his name. It was something Sara could handle herself.

He hooked the desk chair with one boot toe, rolled it over, put his boots up on it and sat and thought about the dark heat he had seen in Sara's beautiful eyes when his shirt had come off. It had flared when she had lowered her gaze and discovered that the fly of his jeans wasn't lying flat anymore. He hadn't meant that to happen. The idea of actually stripping on down and helping Sara do the same had suddenly driven him just about crazy. He couldn't help wondering how deep and strong Sara's heat would run if it were given half a chance.

He was still sitting there after the harness brasses rattled the customer's departure a few minutes later. He was still sitting there when Sara, having let extra minutes go by, peered around the doorjamb and inquired, "Have you recovered your mind yet?"

Look at him, she thought, sitting there relaxed and appearing to be half asleep in the cozy chair big enough for two. Half asleep, maybe, but not drowsy—more like a big jungle cat that could launch itself onto prey in the blink of an eye. He was, without a doubt, the most irritating, unpredictable, difficult man she had ever known. He lounged on his spine, his boots on her chair, scrutinizing her with those mocking granite eyes of his, a smile flirting with his lips. Something was about to come out of his mouth, she could tell. Probably something abominable.

He did not disappoint her. He thoughtfully sucked some air through his teeth, then drawled, "Why don't you come on over here, little Sara, and we'll test whether or not two can fit in this chair, like I said?"

"Owen, quit it."

"Scientific experiment. Shouldn't hinder the progress of science." He hitched over in the chair and patted the five inches of seat beside him. "I can tell right now, little Sara, that sweet little backside of yours is going to fit like—"

"Have you ever heard of sexual harassment in the workplace?"

"A new Parker Brothers game?"

"No!" She edged toward the desk. "I'm taking that walk you suggested." She snatched her jacket and purse from the hook by the desk and made for the doorway, afraid and, for some stupid reason, almost hoping he would lunge up out of the chair and drag her back into it with him. "I would not sit with you in that chair if you came sugar-coated!"

"Little Sara, I may not be sugar-coated, but I do taste sweet. Come taste me."

"On second thought," she choked, "I don't think I'm coming back today." She was so rattled that she tried to shove her right arm into the jacket's left sleeve. "I'll see you on Monday!"

"Sunday, little Sara."

Sunday? The gathering at Haddon's. She paused near the tunnel, struggling with the jacket. "Oh, *shoot*!"

"Don't bring a date, Sara. I've changed my mind about that."

"Take a cold shower, Dixon!" she advised over her shoulder.

"But the bathroom here's a half bath, Sara." His laughing complaint floated into the tunnel after her.

"Make *do*!" she hollered, going out the front door, leaving his laughter and the brasses rattling behind her.

Oh, the cool outdoors felt good! What in the world had made anybody, herself included, think Owen had mellowed? He was still as crazy as ever!

She went down the steps and took the Aunt Ada's shortcut. She desperately needed some strenuous walking, then she'd have a doughnut and something to drink. Maybe by the time she got back Owen would be halfway normal and she would give him the other two hours' work he was entitled to. Maybe by then the hot excitement simmering from her breasts down to her thighs would have cooled off and allow her to function more normally.

The sun hit her in the face and she looked up at its

brilliant fingers. As soon as she was certain Owen could not hear her, she laughed out loud. It was a terrible thing, but she knew now with certainty. Owen was the sexiest, brightest, most annoying man she had ever met. She wanted him. Owen was, and probably had always been, the one and only man for her. Dealing with it would probably hurt like crazy, but, whatever happened, it would be worth it in the long run.

Dear God, she inquired, looking up through the soaring pines, *why did you send me a man like Owen? I could handle Kevin, but I don't have the faintest idea how to handle Devil Dixon.*

The pines just snickered in the breeze.

It snowed lightly Saturday night.

Sitting just under the Mogollon Rim, Payson was expected to receive several snowfalls each winter. Sara was torn between hoping the snow would stop so the Dixon family gathering wasn't spoiled and wanting it to snow until the secondary road leading to Doubtful Ranch would be impassable. After her doughnut, she hadn't gone back to work on Friday, and she almost dreaded seeing Owen again. He would be exultant and disgusting.

On the other hand, she told herself, nothing had really happened. Her imagination had improved enormously since that Halloween night five years before. She knew what *something else* was now. Owen probably didn't even begin to guess that a large part of her wished he had not been interrupted, or that, even now, luscious, delight quivered in her middle and rippled down her thighs when she imagined what might have happened next if the harness brasses hadn't jingled. Owen would probably have gone no further with his little striptease, just laughed at her expression and told her what a prig she was, what a sucker.

He was the sucker and didn't even know it. He didn't

realize how lonely he was. He didn't realize how few real friends he had other than her. He didn't realize how much he needed her. Maybe he didn't love her, but he did need her. She might settle for that.

The snow stopped at 10:00 P.M.

Owen was not in church Sunday morning. Sara's brother made the fifteen-minute drive from there to the turnoff to Haddon's ranch in twenty.

"You drive like such a granny," Sara accused as Robert's pickup rolled into Doubtful Ranch.

Robert was a carbon copy of their father, slightly above medium height, with square shoulders and blunt hands, sandy hair, and a pair of teasing brown eyes. "What are you so antsy about? You're usually glad I drive so sanely."

She denied being antsy, but the truth was that every nerve stood at attention, waiting for her first glimpse of Owen, waiting to see what sort of temper he was in. She knew he and his oldest brother had never gotten along, although she didn't know why—another of the secrets Owen hugged to himself. If he was still in the strange mood he'd been in on Friday, it could be a novel day. It was concern, she told herself, nothing more, that made her scan the ranch so carefully, looking for the tall, lean body that was so familiar and . . . She had almost thought him comfortable. Owen? Comfortable? Ha.

Knowing a veterinary emergency could drag him out into a mud-wrestling match with a horse or steer, Robert had worn decent jeans and a new flannel shirt to church. Sara had worn a straight black wool skirt and heels but had partially changed clothes before they had started for Doubtful Ranch. She still wore the tailored, long-sleeved black satin blouse that had gone so elegantly with the skirt, brightened by a small ruby pin that had been her mother's, but now it was tucked into black jeans. Her hair was still gathered into a knot, softened by curly wisps that flirted with her ears. The style gave her an air of businesslike maturity. It seemed important to have that demeanor when she met the dreaded Older Brother for the first time in years. Maybe it was a good idea to give Owen a suggestion of businesslike maturity, too. Maybe some of it would rub off on him.

Sara already knew Haddon Dixon raised and trained Morabs, a handsome cross between the Morgan and Arabian horse breeds, but because Haddon had acquired it just before she had moved to Phoenix, she had never seen Doubtful Ranch. It was small and neat, hunkered down in a protected, cleared saucer in the forest under the Rim. The white house, two compact stories, squatted to the left of the road on the higher side of the clearing. The drive led to a graveled parking area at its side, then turned back down the hill in a neat oval. Haddon's muddy black four-by-four was parked beside the house. Near it were an unfamiliar white sedan, a vaguely familiar red truck, and alongside that, Owen's pickup.

A porch stretched away on either side of the green front door, with a distant view of the rim. Rock-edged raised flower beds flanked the porch and scooted away around each corner of the house. They were empty now, but Sara could imagine how they might look in the spring, filled with dazzling color. Haddon, she thought affectionately, would be more likely to plant them with hay.

On the other side of the road sprawled a large arena, a hip-roofed barn, and a set of neatly fenced corrals. A couple of pregnant mares, ambling through the pasture toward the barn, pointed curious ears at the pickup. A chestnut horse and a rider in vivid blue circled inside the arena fence at a relaxed lope.

Where the road forked, Robert turned down toward the barn.

"Hey," Sara objected, "why didn't you go to the house?"

"Because the horses are in the barn. Haddon's always been eccentric about keeping them there."

"Are you actually planning to work? It's a party."

Instead of replying, he stopped the truck near the barn door and got out. Resigned, Sara got out, too, and watched him unlock the refrigerated unit that was virtually a permanent part of the pickup bed.

"I'm going to vaccinate a couple of new horses," Robert answered at last. He dropped a small bottle and a couple of alcohol swabs in a jacket pocket and waved a pair of disposable syringes at her. "This way, I don't have to bill Haddon for a trip charge, so he'll be happy—and he's going to give me free food, so I'll be happy. It won't take ten minutes, and we'll all be happy."

Free food. Owen's words, designed to tempt her into attending today's assembly. Was that why he had invited her, so she'd bring Robert so that Haddon could avoid a trip charge? Irritating thought. Turning from the truck as her brother walked into the barn, she watched the horse and rider come around the far end of the arena and start down the rail.

Owen looked so easy on a horse, she thought with a rush of pride. He was natural and economical. It was a shame he didn't keep horses of his own, but he said mere pleasure horses were more trouble than they were worth, and if he felt like straddling a horse, Haddon was obliging.

He had enjoyed rodeoing but had never been better than good at it. Bronc riding was what he would have liked to excel at, but he was too big a man—most of the superb bronc riders were the little, wiry guys who could stick like a burr to the back of an enthusiastic bucker. He hadn't quite had the shoulder strength and weight to be better than a fair steer wrestler, and according to him, he had too much intelligence to ride bulls. He'd become a roper instead, with a good eye, a good technique, and fast down a rope. It hadn't been what he had wanted to do, so he hadn't stuck with it.

Maybe, she thought, watching as the chestnut dropped down into a walk, not sticking with it had always been Owen's problem. He had wanted to be excellent at something and had tried different things, hoping to click with the right one. Maybe he hadn't found the right one until he had inherited the business from his grandfather. He was an excellent hatter. Everyone said so. Was that the right thing? If he was content with that, felt successful and good at it, would he be considering selling the shop?

Maybe it was the same way with women, too. Maybe he kept trying them, one at a time, hoping to find the right one.

She leaned her elbows on the rail. The next time Owen seemed to glance toward her, she waggled her fingers. He lifted one hand in response and promptly angled the chestnut across the damp arena at a flat walk. They reached her in a few moments, and Owen stepped down from the saddle in one enviably lithe movement.

"Hi," she greeted.

"She's speaking to me," he said wonderingly.

She ignored that. "What are you doing out here all by yourself?"

As if prompted, children erupted from the mouth of the barn, chattering, gradually becoming three distinct entities. The oldest were dark boys, one about ten, the other a six-year-old. The youngest was a yellow-haired little girl of four who looked as if she would be lucky to make it across the yard without landing face first in a puddle of melted snow.

Owen propped one hip against a post and nodded toward the children. "If you call that being all by myself, you have a funny perception of solitude. Your brother in the barn?''

She nodded.

''He must've run them out. The two oldest there have convinced gullible Uncle Had'n they have the brains and physical fortitude to ride a horse before dinner. Somehow Uncle Owen drew the duty of taking the edge off this old girl to make sure she behaves herself.'' He tousled the chestnut mare's forelock, then spent the next moments brushing it back into order with his fingertips. ''I'm glad you decided to come, little Sara.''

She shot him an intense brown glare. She was definitely sick of being little Sara. ''I said I would.''

Amusement lurked in his gray eyes. ''After Friday, I wasn't so sure.''

She looked at him from under lowered lashes. ''When it started snowing, I did hope it wouldn't stop.''

He put one hand on the rail and leaned closer. ''The Person who makes the snow fall was on my side, I see. What a nice change.'' He flicked the point of her chin with one cold fingertip. ''Cheer up. I hardly ever strip in front of my family.''

''Owen!'' She glanced around to see that the children had stopped halfway across the yard—the smallest had found something fascinating in the mud.

Owen grinned. ''They couldn't hear a seven-forty-seven taxi by over their own din.''

''Maybe. Kids hear everything except what they're supposed to. Drew's?''

''Yeah. Cute little rug rats. At Drew's age, you'd think his kids would be in college, by now. He got a late start. Why'd your face turn that cute shade of pink when I mentioned stripping, little Sara?''

Little Sara again! It suddenly made her furious. She started to turn away, but he caught her wrist in an iron grip. It wasn't painful, but she knew she wouldn't be able to get free without an undignified struggle. She hissed, "Why do you *call me that all the time*?"

"Because it irks you. It makes your eyes get bright, and mad, and pretty." His eyes coasted down until they reached the black satin collar peeking through her partially unzipped jacket. He released her wrist and moved his hand to her throat. "This's nice." He took the collar between his fingers, savoring the satin. "Like a nightgown. Silky. Cool. Very sexy." He raised his eyes to hers. "Tell me, little Sara, do you sleep in something like this, too? Or do you sleep in nothin' at all?"

Just having his hand there, touching her skin, near her throat, near her breast, made her breath catch painfully. His words fanned a downright lustful flame inside her. His eyes held hers while the seconds ticked by. He knew she couldn't say what she wanted to because the children were near. Instead, she asked with a slight tremble in her voice, "Did you—remember to bring the boxes?"

"They're in my truck. I forgot. . . . Good thing you mentioned them. We'll take them up to the attic later." There was nothing suggestive about his words, but his eyes still relentlessly held hers, looking deeply into them, making her grow warmer and curiously needy feeling, wondering just what he had planned for her in the attic. His thumb tucked itself beneath her collar, the tip of it feeling cold against her soft, warm skin. His fingers slipped down into the *V* of the collar, his knuckles rubbing gently, his fingertips reaching until they lightly scraped against the beginning soft swell of her breast. His touch made her knees weaken and her stomach turn liquid. An entire herd of goosebumps stampeded from his caress, making her breasts suddenly feel full and achy.

He knew, she realized with shy pleasure. He knew what affect he was having on her. The pressure of his hand increased against her skin. His eyes turned hungry.

In slow motion, she reached up and shoved his hand away.

"Uncle Owen, we're ready to ride," the older boy announced loudly. The kids were panting from running. "We got our muscles all warmed up like you said."

Owen shot an ironic glance at Sara. *A ploy to get them out of my hair*, it said. *Keep your mouth shut.* His derisive grin growing, he gave her cheek a quick caress with the back of his hand, then pushed away from the low fence and leaned over to lift the little girl onto the rail.

The boy said, "Louie's too little, Mom said."

"Oh, I don't know," Owen said, tweaking the girl's ear. She grinned shyly and hid her face against his vest. "Louie would like to ride, too, wouldn't you, Louie?" He lifted his eyes to Sara's. "This pretty little lady is my niece, Louisa. The gentlemen are Matthew and Deacon. Fellas, this is Sara. Sara works for me."

Matthew promptly asked, "Are you gonna ride with us?"

"Yeah," Owen echoed mischievously, "are you gonna ride with us? The arena's a mite mushy but safe enough."

"I haven't been on a horse in years," Sara said with a wry smile. "I'd probably get so sore I couldn't move tomorrow, and I have a lot of work to do."

Owen shot her a look. "I give a great therapeutic massage." He pushed his attention back to the children. "Well, who needs her, anyway? Come on, Louie my darlin', up we go."

"You said *we* could ride!" Matthew protested.

"You will," Owen told him. "Let me give the young'un a spin first, then it's your turn."

"Do we gotta ride with *you*? Like *babies*?"

"If you can keep your voice down below a screech and stay outside the fence, you can ride alone."

Owen tossed the little girl across his shoulder like a sack of flour and swung into the saddle to the tune of giggles that didn't stop until he had situated the child in front of him. "Don't be wigglin' or a-kickin' this nice horsie, now," Sara heard him say as he turned the mare in from the rail. He lowered his head, murmuring something else, and another flood of giggles poured from under the yellow curls. When he chose to, Owen could wind even the youngest of women around his finger.

The boys fidgeted around Sara. The smaller boy, who seemed to share some of his sister's shyness, asked wistfully, "Don't we get to ride?"

"He just said we did, stupid," Matthew said with brotherly callousness. "Soon's he's done messing with Louie." He turned his attention to Sara. "Do you know my mom?"

"No, I haven't had the pleasure of meeting her, yet."

"She's fixing a turkey, and the house smells *real* good."

"I'll bet it does."

"We were gonna barbecue, but it's got too cold, Uncle Had'n says. We have a gas barbecue in our yard. It's better than brick ones like Uncle Had'n's. D'you barbecue? We do all the time."

"Sometimes, when the weather's nice. You live in Colorado, don't you?"

"Uh-huh. In Denver. This don't seem cold to us. Denver's a mile high."

Sara didn't bother pointing out that Payson was nearly that, and the elevation of Haddon's place was probably even closer to it.

"My dad's a cop. Do you know my dad?"

"I met him once a long time ago."

"He's a detective. He went to Vietnam and got a Purple Heart for getting wounded. He had shrapnel in both legs."

"I'm sure he was very brave. It takes a lot of courage to serve your country in that way."

"He says 'guts.' My mom says it's impolite. He says it took lots of guts," Matthew repeated with relish. "He says being a cop takes guts, too. He says it don't take guts to ride horses or make hats."

"Does he?" Sara had already acquired a preliminary dislike of Drew from Owen simply by association. She suddenly felt dislike mushroom into something nastier. "I think it takes a different kind of guts," she couldn't help saying. "Doing something well, working at it faithfully, even when you feel sick, or sad, or lonely, takes guts."

Matthew looked at her as if she had spoken in Arabic, then turned his attention to the ambling chestnut mare. "My mom said Uncle Had'n's horses would be pretty. That's a shaggy *old* horse."

Sara explained that the mare would be pretty in the summer when she had shed her heavy winter coat, and she tried to explain the vagaries of equine mentality that made an older, more experienced horse a better mount for children. She got nowhere. Matthew Dixon, she found, had firmly entrenched ideas about a number of things. By the time the chestnut mare had circled the arena twice at an easy trot, she was ready to hang Matthew by his heels and swat some open-mindedness into him. There was obviously a strong streak of stubbornness in the Dixon genes.

Having finished with his chore, Robert walked across to the arena as Owen brought Louie back to them. Sara was performing introductions when Owen rode up to the group. He swung down and set the child on the rail in front of Sara.

"Miss Louisa gots to go," he said, turning a gleaming eye to Sara. "Prob'ly all that jiggling and giggling. How about taking her up to the house?"

"It would be my pleasure. Come with me, Louisa."

Sara held out her arms, but the child just looked at her with wide blue eyes until Owen gave her a little poke in the ribs and said, "Go with Aunt Sara, Louie."

Aunt Sara! Was it worse or better than being little Sara? She shot him a dirty look.

He flashed her a grin before saying "Give me your hand, boy," lifting Deke bodily over the rail by one arm. Deke, like his sister, laughed. Matthew scowled.

"I oughta be next," he said loudly. "I'm the oldest."

"You're also the noisiest. You're the one who didn't want to be treated like a baby. A grown-up would be polite and let his younger brother have a good ride first. Robert, howdy."

Robert shook Owen's hand as Sara started up the slope with Louie clinging to her fingers. She heard Robert inquire impudently what Owen charged for baby-sitting, and Owen responded by beginning to tell a joke about a veterinarian and a lawyer. Sara hoped it was clean enough for small ears, particularly as one set accompanied such a large mouth.

What a shame, Sara thought, walking at Louisa's speed. Owen ought to be a daddy. She had never considered what a good one he might be. She had heard him state any number of times he wouldn't have children. Too much trouble. Too expensive. Too noisy. Too much responsibility. Too limiting. Too confining. Still, he had handled his niece gently and with humor. His obnoxious nephew, too, with patience. . . . Speculating was pointless. There would be no Owen's child.

SIX

The front door of the house thumped and Haddon came down the porch steps. From a distance, as he came across the winter-killed lawn, Haddon might have been taken for Owen. He walked with the same casual ease of motion and wore a similar blue down vest, gray flannel shirt, and wide-brimmed silverbelly hat.

Sara liked Haddon but had never felt as close to him as to Owen. He was a loner, content with the company of his horses and his live-out housekeeper, making an occasional excursion to town or tolerating a visit from a potential customer. Some said he never smiled. All business and no sense of humor. Sara knew otherwise. You had to look for his smile behind the lenses of his gold wire-rimmed glasses.

Haddon's hair was black like Owen's, but his eyes were more blue than gray. A thick black mustache drooped around his mouth, and that, along with the old-style glasses and mule-ear boots he wore, gave him an old-time look. Sara was positive he had no intention of looking antique. He wore what he liked and didn't object to the results.

He waited until he was six feet away before he said,

"Hey." His voice was similar to Owen's, too, with the same interesting, slightly gratey quality. He put out a hand, and Sara's disappeared in its warm, brief grip. "Glad you came. Look at how you've changed."

"I'm glad you let me. I don't think you've changed at all."

"Changed my socks once." His eyes twinkled. He leaned down and lifted Louisa. "Hi, there. What're you two up to?"

Owen probably would have said he'd changed his underwear, then described what he was wearing now, Sara thought wryly. She watched Haddon plant a kiss in his niece's hair, wondering that anyone could find him humorless or unfeeling. "I wouldn't squeeze her too hard, if I were you," she advised. "We were on our way to the, uh, little girl's room."

He promptly passed Louisa into Sara's arms. "Don't let me stop you. Robert come?"

"Yes, he's down with Owen and the boys. He's done the vaccinations. He expects to be well fed for his trouble, too."

"I bet. He bring a date?"

"No. He's on call."

"You bring a date?"

"No," she said, and felt her cheeks ridiculously turning pink, recalling Owen's ordering her not to do so on Friday, and the striptease that had preceded. "I haven't had time to get reacquainted."

"Good," Haddon said cryptically. "I'll go down and make sure Matthew hasn't been strangled."

Sara grinned. "I thought it was just me."

"No," he said solemnly. "Notice his little forked tongue flicking in and out? Inherited it from his father." He paused, looking down toward the arena, then at her. "Might not get another chance to say this. You're doing Owen a world of good."

Surprised, Sara replied, "He wasn't in arrears on his

paperwork as much as he thought. It's been pretty easy, actually."

Haddon shook his head. "Not talking about paperwork. Go on in the house. Bathroom's top of the stairs, left. My brother and his wife are in the front room with Donna and Nick Foley. Know them, don't you?"

"Donna who used to be Donna Woods?"

"That's her. Go meet my brother." His lips twitched, maybe fighting a grin, maybe in annoyance, it was hard to tell. "It's an experience."

He walked away. After half a dozen steps, he called over his shoulder, "We'll eat in about an hour. Hope you like turkey."

"Some of my best friends are turkeys," she called back with a grin, and carried Louisa toward the house.

Haddon's house was a basic "living room on the right, dining room on the left, kitchen in the back, and stairs up the middle" floor plan dating back sixty years. The furniture was comfortable without being shabby, and modern without being avant-garde. If there was a particular design or color scheme, Sara couldn't distinguish it. Haddon, she suspected, had furnished the same way he dressed—with whatever he happened to like. Luckily, what he liked was not unpleasant.

Louisa guaranteed she knew the location of the bathroom and didn't need any help because she was *four*, so Sara let her go bumping up the stairs by herself. There was a full rack of coats in the foyer. She took off her jacket and hung it there, then ventured through the wide, arched entrance to the living room.

The men stood when she entered. Nick Foley, the nearest, greeted her pleasantly. His wife, Donna, a freckled, flaming redhead, had been a year ahead of Sara in high school, not a bosom buddy, but a friend. Nick was a relative newcomer to Payson and ran a feed store, which was probably how he came to be friendly enough with Haddon to have been honored with a rare invitation to his home.

If she had not known he would be here, Sara thought with satisfaction, she would have recognized Drew as a Dixon. He was as tall as the others but beefy shouldered, with arms and hands like big chunks of hard stone. His hair was the same straight black but with white sprinkled through it. He had the same cleanly angled jaw, but his cheekbones were less well defined than his brothers', and above them, his gray eyes were chips of pale flint that his ghostly smile never touched.

Drew's wife was a shock. "A cool little number," Owen had said. Marcy could have passed for a high school senior. Long, silky blond hair fell past her waist. No one, Sara thought sourly, should be allowed to have a waist that small. To emphasize it, the woman wore a jump suit of clinging red wool, belted with a black sash. Aside from those endowments, she had the most beautiful face Sara had ever seen outside of a magazine cover. Perfect, lean cheeks and wide green eyes with natural lashes a mile long. The name *Danielle* flickered in the back of Sara's mind. Apparently the taste for gorgeous blondes also ran strongly in the Dixon genes.

Once introductions had been completed, Drew suggested she take a seat near the couch where he had been sitting with his wife. Something commanding about the suggestion made Sara feel like sitting somewhere else, just to see his expression, but she compliantly sat where he had indicated.

"I understand you work for Owen," he said.

"Yes."

"What do you do for him? I wouldn't have thought he'd need hired help in his . . . line of work." There was something close to a sneer on his lips.

She bit back the urge to say she was Owen's personal masseuse and said, "I'm just there temporarily. He had some things he wanted to get caught up on, so I'm helping out with some correspondence and so forth.''

"You actually type, do you?"

"Ninety words a minute."

"How long have you known him?"

Drew's wife, Sara discovered, had a perfect voice, too. A soft, perfectly modulated Southern accent drifted out of her perfect mouth.

"Don't pay my husband any mind, Sara honey. It's his job to ask questions, and sometimes he forgets he's not on duty." A tiny needle lurked in her last word. Drew cast her a warning look.

"I asked a simple question. I'd like to know how long she's known him."

Maybe some emotion would show in his eyes if she said, "It's none of your business." Instead, she said, "I guess you don't remember me, do you?"

"Is there some reason why I should?"

"Not unless you remember a clumsy girl tripping over your feet and spilling a cup of grape-juice punch down the front of your white dinner jacket at a Christmas concert once." She saw his wife's perfect eyebrows rise and added apologetically, "I was about ten at the time. I burst into tears in the middle of 'O Holy Night.' "

Donna chuckled while recognition and irritation flickered in Drew's flinty eyes. "I remember. Your father paid my cleaning bill. He's a lawyer, is he not?"

"Nothing so lofty. He was a CPA. He died last year. I understand you're a cop."

The term irritated him as much as she could have hoped for. "We prefer that those outside the law-enforcement community use the term 'police officer.' "

"Sorry. Matthew told me his dad was a cop. I didn't realize it wasn't okay to say that."

She didn't know what drove her to irritate the man, but she couldn't seem to help it. To avoid a head-on collision, she turned to Owen's sister-in-law and said, "Matthew told me you're cooking a turkey. It smells fantastic—I could smell it clear outside. Is there anything I can help you with?"

Marcy wafted a languorous hand, drawling, "Why, actually, it's Mrs. Foley who's preparing the turkey. It was pure good fortune Haddon had a turkey put by. He hadn't thought to make a contingency plan in case it snowed this weekend. Men are so like that, aren't they, sugar?" One of her perfect ruby fingernails tickled her husband's ear. He all but jerked his head away from her touch. "Truth to tell, I wouldn't have a notion as to what to do with a turkey, so it was another purely fortunate thing that Mrs. Foley did, or I 'spect we'd be havin' pizza for supper."

"Ah," said Sara neutrally, then turned a desperate eye toward Donna. "Well, then, is there anything I can help you with, Donna?"

Donna looked blank. "Help?" Then the message sank in. She bounced out of the chair she'd been curled up in and said, "Yes! I was about to start a fruit salad and mashed potatoes. You can help me."

Drew's legs, outstretched beneath the coffee table, blocked Sara's path. When he showed no inclination to pull them in, she murmured, "Excuse me," and stepped over them.

"You did that a good deal better than the last time," Drew said softly.

She glanced sharply at him. Had it been Owen, or even Haddon, there would have been a twinkle in his eyes. Instead, there was only wintry flint. If that was his idea of humor, it left her cold.

Sara and Donna managed to be silent until they reached the warm, aromatic kitchen. Once the door swung shut behind Sara, she shuddered and said, "Good thing nobody in there has diabetes. That accent would finish them off."

The redhead struck a pose at the refrigerator. With a breathy accent, she said, "My goodness gracious, I simply haven't the faintest idea how to open this little ol' refrigerator. It—it *is* a refrigerator, isn't it?"

Obligingly, Sara said, "This is an antique model, *Mrs. Foley*. One pulls the handle."

With exaggerated wonder, Donna hooked the handle and pulled. As the seal sucked free and the door swung open, she looked at Sara with wide eyes and said, "Oh, thank you ever so much. You know, I have *always* relied upon the kindness of strangers."

Donna buried her snickers in the vegetable crisper, and Sara stifled hers over the sink.

"A piece of work, that Drew is," Donna said quietly, later. They stood side by side, peeling potatoes and dropping them into a pot of water. "Haddon had given Nick a hint of how miserable he had made their lives growing up. I didn't believe it until today. The man's on a strange trip."

"Owen has said things to me, too. I thought it was, oh, sibling rivalry, or Owen's private war, or something. I felt like smacking Drew's face before one word had come out of his mouth. I wonder how he ever made detective."

"Maybe that chilly façade comes in handy for that sort of work. When he and his partner play good-cop-bad-cop, I bet I know who plays bad-cop. My brother became a cop, did you know? They're not all like that. You know what's weird?"

"What?"

"I get the impression Mrs. Drew loves him, in her own neurotic way, and, really, she's kind of nice. The kids run her ragged. I found myself volunteering to give her a break from them this evening. I'm crazy, I guess, but I love kids."

Sara said noncommittally, "You had a better chance to evaluate them than I did. . . . I was rude, getting up and charging off like that. I was afraid I would say something dreadful—then his eyes would begin to glow a weird orange, you know, and they'd shoot out laser beams and leave me lying on the floor, fried to a crisp.''

Donna's laughter was infectious. Eventually, they calmed and were able to talk old times. The turkey, Sara learned, had not been as impromptu as Marcy had implied. Haddon had stuffed it himself that morning. He had extracted Donna's promise to help him with meal preparation when he had extended his original invitation.

"He's had Nick and me over a couple of times to barbecue, so I owe him. He's actually a pretty good cook,'' Donna said, "but he didn't want to spend the whole day in the kitchen. So's Owen. I guess you know that.''

Haddon inviting people to barbecue? Owen cooking? If she had thought about it at all, she would have assumed Owen ate out most of the time. She realized she had never even seen inside the house he had bought after his grandfather had died. *Good grief.*

"Good grief what?''

Sara hadn't realized she had spoken aloud. "I was just thinking that I've known Owen for years but barely know where he lives.''

"Well, he isn't as bad as Haddon, but he keeps to himself.''

"I've seen his house from the road, of course, but . . . I didn't know he could cook, either.'' She turned speculative eyes on Donna.

Reading her mind, Donna grinned. "Don't look green-eyed at me. Bonnie dated Owen a couple of times. That's the only reason I know.''

Donna's older sister, Bonnie, had married and moved away years before. "I wasn't looking green-eyed,'' Sara said defensively, but she was relieved to know she wasn't standing next to one of Owen's "string," and she did feel a new, faint dislike for Bonnie. "I was only wondering. . . ."

"Right. It was a long time ago."

"It doesn't make any difference to me."

"Right. Oh, for—" Donna grabbed two potholders. "I should have basted that stupid bird fifteen minutes ago!"

The only practical suggestion Marcy had to offer was that the children be fed in the kitchen, allowing them to be noisy and spill on the floor as necessary. This arrangement did not overjoy Matthew. Application to his father for an exemption was denied. Matthew was charged with looking after his sister and brother while the adults ate.

The gleaming walnut pedestal table that had belonged to the Dixon men's grandmother was lovely but, its leaf having gone astray over time, was better suited to seating six than eight. The diners were slightly crowded. When he sat beside her, Owen gave Sara a solemn wiggle of his eyebrows and whispered, "Cozy."

Sara thought it would be like the arrogant older brother to demand the honor of occupying the head of the table. He didn't. Haddon sat at the head, with Owen at his right and Drew to his left. Sara sat on Owen's right, across from Marcy, with Donna to her right. Nick was at the table's foot, flanked by his wife and Robert.

Since Haddon had already carved the turkey to remove the children's portions, starting dinner was a matter of saying grace and passing dishes. Conversation began with a weather discussion. Gradually, Nick and Robert became involved in a debate on feeds and nutrition. Donna complimented Haddon on the stuffing, and he dutifully gave credit to her and Sara for their work in the kitchen. Sara looked at Donna and saw wide eyes full of suppressed laughter. It was all she could do to keep from giggling as she stole a guilty peep at their unwitting victims. Owen frowned, as if he could see sideways, as if he knew they were up to something but didn't know what. His thigh pressed hers, asking what was going on. His blue jeans gently rubbed her black ones. She nearly swallowed an ice cube.

Drew related some interesting aspects of being a homicide detective. Haddon made an occasional comment; Marcy made intermittent remarks designed to steer her husband around some of the less pleasant facets of his job.

Owen said virtually nothing. No jokes about the food, no snide remarks directed at his eldest brother, no disreputable comments at all. What a nice break, Sara thought. Then, as his silence continued, she began to feel uneasy. Covert glances at his profile told her little, except to remind her that it was an excellent, strong profile. He ate slowly, seemed to enjoy what he ate, didn't look at her, even when she asked him to pass the gravy or the strawberry jam, and when a squabble broke out in the kitchen, he was first to toss his napkin down next to his plate and silently go out to put a stop to it. Something was wrong.

When the squalling in the kitchen diminished, Marcy murmured, "My, he does have a knack with the children, doesn't he?"

"Maybe he's finally found his niche," Drew said with heavy irony. "He ought to dump that business of Granddad's and open a day-care center."

Sara froze, a forkful of Haddon's stuffing near her mouth, staring at Owen's brother. He sank his teeth into a drumstick, his frigid glance directed at her over it. For a moment, she glimpsed what it would be like to be a criminal looking down the barrel of Detective Dixon's pistol.

She lowered her fork and said, "Owen is good at what he does."

His eyebrows went up, uncannily like Owen's. "You know," he said with an icy smile, "I'll bet you're not the only woman to say that."

Next to her, Donna gave a tiny gasp. The implication that there was some sexual relationship between Owen and her bothered her less than the fact that the man had so maliciously cut Owen down. She could feel warm blood creep up her neck.

Before she could speak, Haddon quietly said, "Sara works for Owen."

"So she said. So he told me. People tell me a lot of things in my line of work. Doesn't mean I believe everything I'm told."

Haddon, still quietly, said, "You're out of line."

Drew took another bite of turkey and chewed it slowly, after which he said, "Okay. Owen says she works for him. She says she works for him. You say she works for him. I guess she works for him."

Marcy murmured something that was ignored by her husband. He sat looking across the table at Sara, a challenge in his eyes.

"Owen is an excellent hatter," she said softly. "He has a superb, national reputation for service and fine craftsmanship."

Drew's expression was nearly a smirk. "Impressive. Unsolicited testimony from an *employee* always means so much."

Amazed at her own courage, Sara opened her mouth to reply, but she heard Owen coming back from the kitchen. If he were to hear his brother return an insult, the fur would fly. The atmosphere was already unstable enough. Instead of telling Drew what a self-centered, egotistical jerk he was, she shoved stuffing into her mouth.

Drew looked her in the eye and smiled.

"Everything's fine," Owen said, sliding back into

his place. "The mashed potatoes just blend right in with the ceiling."

"Thanks," Haddon said dryly.

"Thank you, Owen," Marcy said. "I'm pleased the children have taken to you."

He made a little dismissive gesture with his fork, his arm brushing Sara's. "Heck, I just treat them like I should have been treated when I was a kid. Like my grandmother would have is what I mean."

The air at the brothers' end of the table suddenly felt like lightning had struck, leaving behind multiple sharp charges of electricity. Sara stole a sidelong look at Owen. He was slowly putting a forkful of potatoes into his mouth. His eyes were locked on his brother across the table. Drew had put down the drumstick and wiped his hands on his napkin, and simply sat contemplating Owen's face in the table's abrupt, heavy silence.

A sudden frantic chirping sounded from Robert's corner of the table. He groaned, making a grab for the beeper on his belt.

"I knew it was too good to last. I was about to ask what was for dessert, too." He pushed back from the table and stood. "Excuse me. I need to use the phone."

Drew's laugh was a soft, humorless breath. He murmured, "Saved by the bell, little brother."

"Yeah," Owen agreed, deliberately obtuse. "Lucky Robert."

"Will you take me home if he has to leave?" Sara murmured to Owen.

"Sure. Cost you ten bucks."

Donna gave two foil-wrapped pieces of her chocolate fudge cake to Robert as he raged about the damage that barbed wire could do to a panicked horse. If Sara had known what direction the evening was going to take, she would have insisted on two foil-wrapped pieces of chocolate fudge cake for herself and left with him.

The rest of the meal was more of the same strange

dream. After Robert had gone, the others sat around the table, eating the rich, gooey cake and vanilla ice cream, drinking coffee, and manufacturing conversation. There was no better term for it than that. Haddon and Owen were nearly silent—this was normal only for Haddon. Everyone else formed a latticework of low-key remarks and observations. Drew frequently turned heavily ironic eyes on Owen but did not speak to him. If Owen was aware of that, he appeared oblivious as he listened to the conversation. Sometimes Drew's flinty glance settled on Sara, and she could almost hear its message spoken aloud. He lay in ambush, like a cop on a stakeout—or a panther on a limb, waiting until he could pounce and sink in his teeth at the base of the skull.

Sara shivered and unconsciously edged closer to the warmth of Owen's body. He looked sharply at her, the first time he had looked directly at her since the beginning of the meal. The concern in his eyes drew a wistful smile from her. The concern melted into amusement before he turned his eyes back to his coffee.

Eventually, the troublesome dream ended. The men took the boys down to the barn to feed and settle the horses for the cold night. While Sara and Donna washed the dishes—Marcy would have been delighted to help, but her poor, delicate hands simply could not *abide* dishwater—Marcy took Louisa upstairs to have a bubble bath and get ready for bed.

The men and boys invaded the entryway as Sara and Donna finally left the kitchen. Somehow—Sara was never quite sure whose idea it was—she and Donna wound up committed to getting Deke and Matthew cleaned up and ready for bed while the men had coffee and drinks downstairs.

"Aw, *Dad*," Matthew complained, "it's early! I don't have to go to bed yet."

Drew tolerantly ruffled the boy's hair and said, "Watch TV afterward, if you want to."

"I'd rather play a game on Uncle Had'n's computer."

"All right, if he says so."

Standing aside, Sara bent her head toward Haddon and whispered, "Have you actually stepped into the computer age?"

A smile twinkled in his eyes. "You'd be surprised how a computer can simplify horse management. And I don't see anything to grin about."

She sobered promptly. "Neither do I. Only, if your horses play computer games, they must be a marvelous advance in breeding techn—" She ducked a teasing swipe of his hand and herded a griping Matthew up the stairs.

Donna had started the bath water and was persuading Deke out of his clothes. Matthew violently declined assistance with his, so Sara shamelessly abandoned him to explore the rest of the second floor. The three bedrooms were furnished in the same comfortable, haphazard fashion as the downstairs. A smaller one had been converted into an office, where Haddon's computer sat silently under plastic covers.

She found Marcy curled up on what she assumed was Haddon's double bed, reading a book to a nightgowned Louisa while the child lay with her head hanging off the edge of the bed, her curly locks dangling toward the floor.

"The men are finished feeding. Donna's getting Deke into a bath." She twisted her head to get a proper look at Louisa's red face.

"That's so sweet of Donna." Marcy saw Sara's expression and gave a lazy laugh. "Isn't she a caution? It's her favorite position. She'll have the best complexion in the country, if my mama's old saw about letting the blood feed your face is worth anything."

Thinking all Louisa needed for a terrific complexion

was properly working genes, Sara sat beside Louisa and tickled her tummy until she rolled over, giggling. "If you'd like to go downstairs and visit, we could finish up with the kids."

Marcy's long lashes veiled her eyes. "I wouldn't dream of letting you do that." She shook her head, her silky hair rippling over her shoulder, and said frankly, "Drew's in one of his moods. I'd as soon stay up here as be with Drew when he's in one of his moods. He's the best husband a woman could want, but there are times when I'd sooner pretend I don't know him."

If that were the case, Sara wondered at her description of the man as "the best husband a woman could want," but she supposed there had been times her own mother had wanted to let on that her father was a complete stranger, too. She tried to remember . . . but she had been too small when her mother had died.

Marcy added curiously, "I suspect Owen's that way, too, isn't he?"

Owen? Moody? Sara almost laughed. The minor irritation of having everyone think she and Owen had something going that would allow her to know him so intimately kept her from it. "I don't know. What are you reading?"

"*Curious George!*" Louisa bounced up from her dangling position. "Finish the story, Mommy!"

Full of good food and reluctant to move, Sara lay across the foot of the bed, next to Louisa, and echoed sleepily, "Finish the story, Mommy."

Marcy's voice might be too syrupy for normal conversation, but when she read the simple child's story, with much inflection and drama, it was effective. Sara nearly dozed, watching Louisa's mobile face as her mother read, wondering if it was possible that she might produce a child as taking as this one. Genetic dominance was strange. If Sara married someone dark—dark haired and dark complected—would her own dark gold hair be dominant or recessive? Would their children be fair or dark?

It was an insignificant point, of course. Kevin had been dark, but because he had dumped her—the thought didn't bother her so much now, since her talk with Owen—she would have to find a man first, an easy task for someone like Marcy, she suspected, but not for her. Owen—not Owen. Certainly not Owen. He was surely attractive enough, and so would his children have been, but what was the point in wondering? Sara and Owen would not have children together.

Perhaps it was thinking about the man that made her tune in to what was happening where he was. Perhaps it was only that her dinner had settled and its aftermath of drowsy unawareness had passed. Whatever, eventually Sara realized she could hear the men's voices coming up from downstairs, louder than they had been.

Sara glanced at Marcy. She knew, Sara thought. She had heard it, too, but she wasn't about to admit it, because Drew was *in a mood* and she wanted no part of it. She read on without a pause, that silky voice keeping Louie enthralled. Maybe it was best, anyway, if it kept the child from noticing the argument that was going on downstairs.

Sara slipped out of the room, tucking her slinky black shirttail into her jeans, quietly leaving Marcy and Louisa to Curious George's mercy. She managed to step on every creaky place in the stairs as she went down. She expected the voices in the living room to fall silent at the sounds, but perhaps their owners were too involved to pay attention to creaks in an old house full of creaks.

She did not plan to eavesdrop, but once she heard her own name it was impossible to simply step into the room as she had planned. She paused in the entry hall shadowed by twilight, just out of the bath of light that flooded from the arched door of the living room. She hadn't heard the remark Drew must have made, but she did hear the anger underlying deliberate amiability as Owen replied, "Leave Sara out of this. She hasn't anything to do with this."

"You brought her into it," Drew replied. "You brought her here."

"I brought Nick and Donna here," Haddon said with soft derision. "I don't hear you making snide remarks about them. Or Sara's brother. I suppose you think because I invited Nick, Donna, and Robert here that we're all sleeping with one another."

"Wait a minute!" Nick protested. "It's my *wife* you guys are talking about."

"Just making a point," Haddon soothed.

"Well, make it with some other guy's wife."

Ice cubes dropped into a glass, then Drew's voice came. "Refill, Haddon?"

The mundane offer, coming in the middle of the rancorous conversation, astonished Sara. Common civility mixed with venom?

"No, thanks," Haddon said. "I've had enough."

"Nick? How about you?"

"No, thanks. I'm driving."

Glass clinked again. Liquid sloshed. "Owen? Something?"

"I'm stuffed to the gills."

Ice tinkled in liquid. "Of course, I should have remembered. A booze hound like you has to keep a pretty tight rein on himself. Must be murder, having to pass up a free drink."

"I haven't taken a drink, free or any other kind, for years. Bet a nickel you can't say the same."

"Don't let it make you uncomfortable. I understand. I saw a lot of guys like you when I worked vice. Of course, most of them were stretched out cold on the sidewalk."

"Kind of ironic, isn't it?"

"What?" Haddon asked.

"Them letting a high roller like Drew work vice. You'd think they'd worry that a man so anxious to get his hands on other people's money might be tempted to take something under the counter. They call it 'on the take,' in your trade, don't they? 'On the pad?' Somethin' like that."

"I do not accept money on the side," Drew said dangerously. "That's all that ever seems to interest you. Money."

"*Me?* You're the one who's been dancin' around, shovin' money into the conversation for the last twenty minutes. I can't remember the last time I had a conversation with you when we didn't talk about it. You want to talk about the money? Fine! Let's talk about the money and get it out of the way. You got a memory like a wounded elephant."

"When a man's family turns on him, it generally stays with him."

Sara heard a small, derisive snort she thought came from Haddon. Owen said, "I see you didn't make detective because of some enormous improvement in your perceptive powers. Nobody turned on you. You had a stupid idea. The rest of us were bright enough to know it."

There was silence. Then Sara heard someone slowly walking on the wood floor. Drew. Ice tinkled in his drink as he moved. When he finally spoke, his tone was acid. "It was not a stupid idea. It was sound. It could have been a tremendous success! If Granddad hadn't been so tightfisted, I could have returned your money to you twenty years ago, with enormous interest! You were fools—all of you—not to let me do it!"

"Granddad was death on a gamble."

"It was no gamble. It was a sure thing."

Even unable to see his face, Sara knew Owen was wearing his mocking grin. "I'd think a homicide cop'd know what the only sure thing is. It was the longest shot in creation. That's what always made you being a vice cop so funny.''

"You have a lousy sense of humor.''

"I made mine up from pieces of yours when you dropped it. It was a *bad idea*, Drew.''

"Don't bother,'' Haddon said wearily. "You'll talk your tongue down to the root and he'll still smile and say he could have made us all rich.''

Owen went on as if Haddon hadn't spoken. "That money was our future. You'd have lost every penny of it.''

Drew suddenly swore, and Sara heard his glass thump against a hard surface, the ice jingling merrily. "What difference would it have made in the long run? Look what you did with your shares when you grew up. Haddon sank his into a piece of land too small to develop into anything and a bunch of broken-down horses. And, you! You spent yours on rodeo competitions you couldn't win, motorcycles that were on some cop's hot sheet, and twenty women you laid and left! You might as well have burned it!''

"Was it really *twenty* women?'' Owen murmured.

Drew made a loud, exasperated sound. "Why don't you *grow up?*''

"You mean instead of growing down?''

Poor Nick, Sara thought, trapped in there with three loathsome tomcats. Two, anyway—Haddon seemed to be the voice of reason and had spoken more than anyone would have expected from him. Why didn't Nick make some excuse and slip out? Maybe he was enjoying it. Men were funny about such things.

"Anyway,'' Owen added reasonably, "you spent your share your way. We spent ours our way. I don't know how it could have been fairer than that.''

"Fairer!'' Drew's voice went up a couple of decibels. "I should have known you'd end up with a warped sense of fairness, being brought up by that niggardly, selfish old man!''

"Let it go, Drew!" Owen said sharply. "Let it *go!* It's been an eon! Forget what you might have had and get on with your life!''

"How am I supposed to forget? Tell me how I'm supposed to do that!" Drew's voice was loud and harsh. "What do you think I think about every time I look at another hacked-up body? What do you think I think about every time it's time to buy my kids' school supplies, or an anniversary present for my wife? I think about what my life was supposed to be, and I *know* who it was that guaranteed I'd be looking at a flat checkbook and haunted by corpses for the rest of my life! Forget? You don't know what you're talking about!''

"I can talk about something I do know about." Owen's voice was suddenly hushed, dangerous. "You want to talk about dead bodies—being haunted? I'll tell you what haunts *me.*''

"That's enough," Haddon said, but Owen rode on over him.

"What haunts me is seeing my grandmother lying dead on the stairs. My grandmother, Drew. *Our* grandmother. I know she didn't mean diddly to you, but she meant something to me!''

"What are you doing? Blaming me?''

"You're so clever.''

Sara thought for a moment her heart had stopped. She knew she hadn't drawn a decent breath in several minutes. Maybe Drew's breath was hard to find for a moment, too. There was silence. Then his reply came, furious and thunderous.

"She was a fat, old woman! She climbed the stairs too fast and her heart stopped! I had nothing to do with it!''

"You murdered her—as sure as if you'd shot her with your trusty service revolver.''

SEVEN

Her mind reeling with the confusing, acrimonious accusations, Sara sucked in an overdue breath and rounded the corner, through the arch, into the living room.

It was almost like a snapshot. A fire flickered indolently in the fireplace behind Drew. Owen sat on the couch, his back to her. Nick slouched in a chair in the corner, with both Drew and Owen between him and the hallway, leaving him no easy way out of the room if he wanted one. Haddon, deep in another chair, slowly raised his head and looked at her without seeming to see her—but that might have been a trick of the light reflecting off his glasses.

Her voice failed on the first attempt. She would have loved to run then, but this wasn't for her. It was for the little ones. She cleared her throat and said quietly, "The children can hear you."

Drew spun toward her. He was so colossally angry that his face was deeply flushed. His hand was clenching a nearly empty highball glass so hard that she expected it to explode from the pressure.

"I suggest," he said through clenched teeth, "that

128

if the children can hear us, you hike your fanny back upstairs and close some doors.''

That was supposed to be the end of it, she knew. He had spoken, and he did not expect any discussion about it. Marcy would have murmured a gentle admonition and marched dutifully back up the stairs.

With a glance at Owen, Sara said, ''Unless you— gentlemen—intend to modulate your voices, I don't think closing the doors will do the trick.''

''Owen.'' Drew swiveled his head toward his brother, his words snarling across the space between them. ''If you've got any control over this little slut of yours, get her out of my face!''

Owen's lean body launched off the couch so abruptly that even Drew's professional instincts didn't warn him in time. Two catlike steps and a solid, ruthless right to the mouth, and Drew was slammed back against the brick of the fireplace. His glass and ice cubes flew toward Haddon, who batted them aside like pesky flies as he came up out of his chair. Nick shot to his feet, then froze in his corner as if he couldn't decide what to do next.

Drew's surprise lasted just long enough for Owen to land that first punch. Bellowing furiously, he pushed off from the hearth, dropping a shoulder and ramming it into Owen's belly. His momentum carried them both halfway across the room. They crashed onto the couch, Owen grunting under the impact of Drew's fly- ing weight. Drew lifted up far enough to send an awk- ward but effective punch into the side of Owen's face with a sickening sound. Owen grabbed handfuls of his brother's hair and shirt, heaved, and rolled them both onto the floor, sending the coffee table skidding away, drink glasses, coffee cups, and horse magazines flying.

There wasn't much science to it after that. Sara was strongly reminded of a grade school playground fight, with the grunting, rolling bodies and flailing arms. She said, "Oh, honestly!" and Haddon sent her a small grin.

Then Drew was pushed down ferociously. His head hit the floor with a sharp thud. Dazed for a moment, and with Owen's knee pinning his arm to the floor, he couldn't defend against Owen's hands when they wrapped around his throat.

Seconds passed. Drew would break free any moment. He had superior shoulder and arm strength and was a trained police officer. Any moment, now, he would fling Owen's hands aside and roll free. . . .

Sara saw Drew's face begin to change color, his eyes bulge with the strain.

"Owen, stop!" She wanted to scream it, but only a tight whisper would come out as she scrambled around the end of the couch. She couldn't understand why Haddon seem unconcerned, or why Nick, there in his corner, eyes wide open, only watched. Did they really think this was just a brotherly tussle?

Sara went to her knees beside the struggling men, her hands going around Owen's right arm. The overwhelming power and rigidity of the muscles beneath her fingers drew a desperate moan from her. She would never be able to pull him away. He would strangle his own brother before her eyes.

Drew's left hand clawed and cuffed Owen, trying ineffectively to break his hold. Owen's eyes were slitted down to nothing with concentration, while Drew choked, gasped, and turned a terrible, suffocating color.

"Stop," Sara said. "Owen, *stop!*" She hugged the unyielding arm to her body. "Owen, stop!"

Haddon was on the other side now, pulling at Owen's other arm. "Owen, you big fool. Ease off."

Sara threw her arms around Owen's solid body and put her mouth against his ear. *"Owen!"* It was just a whimper. "Owen—let *go!*"

He gave a huge gasp, as if returning from a long

time underwater. His grip eased. She dragged his hand from his brother's throat. Haddon did the same on the other side, while Owen looked at her as if she were some kind of alien being. His chest heaving, his mouth seeping ugly blood, he straightened, then staggered up. He looked down at his prostrate brother, gasped, "You've got *lousy* manners," and walked straight out through the archway. The front door slammed behind him.

Drew coughed a groan and rolled onto his side, sucking in air. For the first time, Sara realized Donna was there next to her husband, looking dazed. Nick finally unfroze and pried Donna's fingers from his arm, coming to squat down beside them and look critically at Drew's face. Haddon put a hand on his brother's shoulder and asked, "All right?"

Drew, coughing, croaked, "Right."

Nick said happily, "That was excellent."

Haddon glanced around at the shambles of his living room. "Best this room ever saw, anyway."

Sara looked from Haddon and Nick to Donna in amazement. Her heart was still pumping at ninety miles an hour, her stomach knotted and sick, but Nick grinned and Haddon calmly began picking magazines off the floor. *Men!*

"*Is* he all right?" she asked doubtfully, as Drew sat up, groaned, and coughed again.

Haddon glanced at her, a faint smile in his eyes. "He will be in a minute. Maybe you ought to go and make sure everything's okay upstairs."

She glanced into the hallway. Marcy must have heard the shouting and flying furniture. Why hadn't she come downstairs to see what was happening? Because her husband performed this way so often that she was inured to it?

She went out through the archway. The first thing

she saw was Owen's coat hanging on the peg rack behind the door.

Behind her, Donna asked, "Sara, are you okay?"

"I'm fine," Sara lied, feeling weaker and more frightened than she had during the brawl. "You should probably go let Marcy know that Drew's all right."

"Marcy didn't seem interested one way or the other," Donna replied dryly. "She started reading another book to Louisa and Deke as if they were on a nice Caribbean beach. Maybe you should sit down."

"I can't," Sara said. With a shaking hand, she retrieved her jacket from a peg near Owen's and slipped into it. She reached for Owen's jacket and discovered his vest underneath it, so she took that, too. "I'll be fine."

"Are you leaving?" Donna sounded apprehensive.

"No. I don't know," Sara murmured, and went out the front door.

The chilly air smacked her face, helping to clear away her nausea. It was quite dark now. The security lights at the barn and above the parking area were already on. In the pool of light at the end of the house, she saw Owen's pickup parked next to the Foleys' Bronco on the gravel turnaround. She stood on the front porch, trying to decide where, in this unfamiliar territory, Owen might go. He was hurt. She had seen blood on his mouth. Still, he had been able to walk away. He might have gone anywhere, to the barn, or into the forest—anywhere. Experimentally, she said loudly, "Owen?"

Silence.

After a moment, she heard a small, familiar sound. Water running. Something like someone sprinkling the lawn, around the side of the house.

A line of flagstones took her around the corner. That side of the house was dark except for light that shone out from the living room by way of the dining room window. She could see Owen there, doubled over.

She sighed with mixed relief and dread. When she drew closer, she heard the trickling of water and realized he was sitting on one of the rock-edged flower beds, drinking water from a spigot at the side of the house. She heard him swish water in his mouth and spit. Maybe *drinking* wasn't exactly the right word.

She stopped, looking down on wet, black hair gleaming in the pale yellow light. She wanted to beat him and tell him what an idiot he was, not to mention how much he had terrified her. She wanted to hug him, kiss every hurt part of him, tell him how much she loved him, how precious he was to her. Instead, outwardly calm, she said, "I thought maybe you'd left."

"I was going to, until I remembered I had to take you home."

"I wouldn't have minded—Donna and Nick would have taken me. I didn't want you driving around in this condition."

"I'm in very good condition. I'm in particularly excellent condition." He scooped another handful of water and rinsed his mouth again. The faucet handle squeaked when he turned it off.

"You were bleeding."

"My cheek got shoved into my teeth. A couple of days, I won't know anything happened to it. Go away, Sara. I'm not interested in *comfort*, right now."

She felt like punching him. He'd said he knew she cared about him. Did he think she could have watched that nasty scene untouched? Didn't he have the faintest idea how she felt about him? She said, too loudly, "How about your jacket? Are you interested in your jacket?" She held it out in one hand, the vest in the other. "Or would you rather just freeze to death? Not a completely unacceptable idea to me right now."

After a moment, he gave a soft, amused hiss, and

stood, blocking the light, taking the coat. She offered the vest, too, but he shook his head, slowly sliding his arms into the coat sleeves.

"Thanks."

"Haddon says Drew is all right."

"Golly gee, I was shifting from one foot to the other, wondering."

About one more sarcastic remark and she would bash the other side of his face for him. What was *wrong* with him, anyway? She had disbelieved when people had said Devil Dixon was crazy, or possessed, or both. What could make a man hate his brother so much that he would . . . ? She shied away. She knew Owen. She *knew* him. She had enough faith in him to know he was not a killer.

Then he shook that faith by savagely running ten fingers through his hair and muttering, "I hate him. *I hate him!*"

He turned slightly, and the light from the window fell across Sara. The confusion and fear on her face touched his heart. He had known today could get nasty. He'd invited her for purely selfish reasons, just to make himself feel more protected. When had he become such a creep, anyway? He dragged in a huge breath, designed to calm himself down. He squeezed her shoulder.

"Poor little Sara. You don't even know what it's all about, do you?"

She shook her head.

"Makes it hard to decide which side to take, doesn't it?"

"What makes you think I'm taking any side?"

"You didn't come out here to sightsee, did you?" He gave her shoulder another squeeze and started down the slope of the lawn toward the driveway.

She watched him go, still confused and afraid. She had never seen so much anger in anyone. She had never seen genuine hatred.

He seemed steady enough on his feet. She followed him to his pickup. He patted his pockets, then leaned his elbows on the pickup's hood and said a tacky word.

Alarmed, Sara slipped a hand around the bend of his arm. "What's the matter? Are you dizzy?"

He gave a half laugh and shook his head. "I've lost my keys. I 'spect they're inside on the floor somewhere."

She sighed with relief. "Haddon was picking things up. I'll get them."

He tensed his arm, pinning her hand against his body. "Sara—forget the keys."

He wanted her to stay with him. She felt a surge of warmth partially disperse the irritation she felt over the fight. Being close to him felt good, even with their jackets insulating the touch of their bodies. She could have worked her hand free from next to his ribs. Instead, she curled it around his arm and moved nearer, until her cheek was almost against his shoulder. In the beam of the floodlight on the end of the house, his hair gleamed darkly.

"Your hair is wet," she whispered. "You'll catch your death."

"It got splashed when I doused my face." He turned baffled eyes on her. "What is it with you? You have a compulsion to mother-hen me! I've always been your missionary project. I've tried for years to make you understand this—you can get hurt by being on my side! Didn't you learn anything just now?" A little jerk of his head said he meant the fracas inside.

"I thought you invited me here because you *wanted* somebody on your side! What was that ruckus supposed to be? A demonstration to make little Sara see what a dastard Owen Dixon is?"

He lowered his head to rest on his forearms atop the hood. "Language, little Sara. *Shame.*"

"I said 'dastard,' with a *D* as in *dog*. It was supposed to be funny."

Sara found herself gently rubbing his back. She didn't know when she had begun, but her hand moved slowly over him. It was rather impersonal, so much jacket between her hand and his body, but doing it made her feel better, and he didn't object. She wasn't even sure he noticed. "Anyway, maybe," she said softly, "some things are worth a little hurt."

"Yeah, right." His skeptical voice sounded hollow, bouncing off the hood. "Name three."

"Okay." She thought for a moment, looking up. There was too much interference from the floodlight, but she knew the sky was cloudless, dotted with distant celestial things. "Important surgery. Having a tooth filled. Having a baby."

He raised his head but didn't look at her. "Men will never be able to understand that. Having a baby. They can understand the mechanics but not that particular pain." He turned to her. "Would you like that, Sara? To have children?"

When his head moved, she could see that his jaw was swelling. She wanted to reach out and touch it gently, but his remark about her being a mother hen kept her from it.

"I'd as soon skip the pain part, but—yes. With the right man. Under the right circumstances. I'm not one of those women who feels she's not A Woman if she can't pop a couple of babies out into the overcrowded world."

His eyes roamed her face in the unflattering light. After a moment, he murmured, "Why do you wear your hair like that?"

Her hand went up involuntarily. "Like what? Is it a mess?"

He gave a quiet snort. "No, it's not a mess. It's so perfect it looks like it was glued on hair by hair. Except for the bangs, and these sideburns." He reached over and flicked one of the wisps.

"They are not *sideburns!* It's a dignified, professional style. It's cool in the summer."

"You may have noticed the snow on the ground this morning."

"It keeps my hair off my face."

"When you were yelling in my ear in there—"

"I wasn't yelling. I'd have liked to be, believe me, but I wasn't yelling."

"When you were whispering sweet nothings in my ear in there, your hair tickled my ear, and when I looked at you, I expected it to be down, loose, like you've been wearing it. I knew it wasn't . . . but I expected to see it that way. That was very weird."

He fell silent, staring at her in the harsh, bare light. His eyes appeared to be distant. She had the feeling he wasn't even seeing her. She said softly, "Maybe you ought to tell me about it."

He blinked and focused on her. "If I do, I'll get mad again. I don't know that I'll survive another adrenaline rush like the last one."

"Maybe you won't get mad. Maybe it will help." She gave his back a small, encouraging pat. "I won't tell anyone."

He looked offended. "I never thought you would, Sara. You say some of the stupidest things I've ever heard. . . ." He put his head on his arms again. She didn't know if he was hiding his expression or simply weary. It was a few moments before he spoke in a deep, dramatic tone: "I was a mama's boy."

"What?"

She felt, rather than heard, a small laugh inside his body. "Well, that's what they called me. I was sick when I was little—a lung infection that wouldn't respond to treatment—and just about died. Afterward, they kept me out of school for a year. My mother and I got very close during that time. I became way too dependent on her."

"She loved you."

"Mmm. You know what happened to my folks?"

"A car accident, wasn't it? Up on the rim?"

"Hit black ice and slid off into thin air. I was barely ten when we moved in with our grandparents. They were already in their seventies—their own children had been grown for better'n thirty years. They liked their solitude. They resented us; we felt it. Granddad sure didn't try to hide it. He left no doubt he was just doing his duty. Grandma—she was, like Drew said, a big woman. Not roly-poly, but big, like some handsome Slavic peasant woman. She wasn't real—loving, but she wasn't mean. She was tired, I think. Managing two kids full-time was more than she was up to."

"Don't you mean three kids?"

"Drew'd been more or less on his own already—he was almost twenty. When Mom and Dad died, he lit out."

"I never realized he was that much older. I'll bet his going made you feel—"

"Like it couldn't have happened too soon. We'd been his personal body servants for years, and Dad let him get away with it. First-born son and all that garbage.

"Drew was born with a mercenary soul, and when he found out about the money, he came back in a flash to"—Owen lifted his head for a moment, and his voice was heavy with sarcasm—"relieve the grandparents of the burden of our care."

"What money?"

"From my folks. My dad didn't have much, just a little ranch out toward Gisela—"

"I know."

"Well, he must've been savin' for something. New herd bull, truck, maybe. Nobody knew. A little money, not much, turned up in a savings account.

"Granddad sold the ranch, and there was some

money from that. Then he put in a couple thousand of his own money. The total wasn't much, would hardly buy a kid's college textbooks today, but it was for our future. He set it up so we could each have our third when we came of age, but before that, not without his permission. I don't know who told Drew—Payson was smaller back then, and word got around better than now. He came boppin' back all smiles and helpfulness and, before long, asked Grandad for the money.''

"And he wouldn't give it to him?''

"Oh, Granddad was happy to give him his third. I 'spect he thought Drew'd take off with it and be out of his hair. Thing was, Drew didn't just want his. He wanted ours. He wanted it all.''

"I knew I didn't like him. What pure selfishness!''

"Depends on your point of view.''

A horse squealed, and Owen raised his head and stared off toward the barn. "He wanted to invest the whole thing in a gun shop. He'd always been crazy about guns. He knew about guns, but he wasn't an expert, he wasn't a gunsmith, and he was just nineteen! A shop like that had been tried, a couple of years before, and had failed miserably, but when you reminded him of that, he had all these excuses for why it had failed—mistakes he wasn't going to make. It wasn't going to work. Everybody knew it but Drew. . . . You couldn't tell him anything. He kept at Granddad until I dreaded to see him coming because I knew there'd be a fight. He'd come late at night, after Haddon and I were in bed, and pester Granddad until they ended up screaming at each other. I can't tell you how many times I woke up to that music in the dark.''

Sara's heart ached to think of that little boy, craving a mother's love and companionship, frightened of his own brother, resented by his grandfather. Sara wanted to put her arms around him to offer comfort, but she knew it wouldn't be welcome. She continued to slowly, lovingly move her hand over his back.

"Sometimes," Owen continued, his voice lowering, "I'd manage to sleep through most of it, until I heard my grandmother come up the stairs and go into their room. She'd be crying. It always seemed strange to think of her crying. She was big and sturdy-looking, like she'd be invulnerable. . . . One night, she came up to get away from them, and her heart just quit. I heard her fall. I got up and went down. I had to climb . . . over her to get down to the kitchen. I had to . . . *scream* to get them to hear me say . . . come and help."

Now Sara did put her arm around him and hug him hard. "It's okay," she whispered. She felt him shudder.

"Drew got drafted, right after that. Haddon and me were left there with the old man. . . . He blamed us. If we hadn't come, Drew wouldn't have come, and Grandma wouldn't have died."

"That's not true."

"No, but that's the way his mind worked. He did keep us. He gave us food, clothing, and shelter. And that is all. That is all."

"No love."

"I would have settled for an occasional smile."

"He left you the shop."

"It didn't matter who got it, as long as someone kept it going. I know in my heart that if anyone else in the family had shown interest in the shop, he'd have left it to them instead of me. If Drew'd been smart, he'd have pretended to like hats instead of guns, then converted. But that would have taken patience, somethin' Drew's short on."

Some things were clearer now. Sara remembered what Owen had said a couple of days before, about having joined the biker gang deliberately so that his grandfather would be annoyed. A boy who was close

to his mother had had her snatched from him. The poor
substitute for her love and attention, his grandmother,
had been taken from him. He had wanted love but gotten duty from his grandfather, and had spent nearly
twenty years trying to pay the old man back by doing
everything he knew would make Benjamin hate him.
Little by little, his family had been chipped away by
death or bitterness, until there was no one left but Haddon. His wild young friends and their silly stunts had
made him feel alive, made him laugh when there was
nothing to laugh about, and brought him some attention
and admiration. He loved the shop but knew it hadn't
been given out of love. Danielle and all the women
before her—he looked for love everywhere, Sara
thought miserably, but couldn't see it right under his
nose.

"Why haven't you ever told me?"

He shook his head. "You may have noticed there's
not a lot in that story to be proud of. . . . Anyway,
it's. . . ."

He hesitated, and she supplied, "Hard for you to tell
anyone your deep, dark secrets."

"I guess."

"I thought maybe I was . . . an exception. I'm not
actually as conceited as that sounds."

"Snob. Egotist. You *are* an exception, Sara."

"Am I? Have you ever—" She could barely finish.
"Told Danielle?"

He looked around at her as if she had asked if he
had ever put a watermelon up his nose. "You know
more about me than any one living person, I swear.
That doesn't mean you know everything. You shouldn't
know everything. . . . I've dated Danielle a few times,
Sara. *That's all.* I haven't told her any secrets, and I
haven't had her—not for want of *her* trying, but she
doesn't interest me enough." He directed a look at her.

"Do you know what I'm talking about? I can put it more plainly, if you don't."

She nodded, shyly hiding her eyes from his, wondering if it was true and ashamed of doubting his words. "Then . . . why did you try to make me think you and she—you know. In your grandfather's chair."

A smile flickered on his lips. "Let's call it a scientific experiment."

"To show what?"

He glanced askance at her. "To see whether or not you were jealous."

Her chest tightened slightly. "And?"

Again the flicker of smile. "I think you could call the experiment a moderate success."

"What—what difference did it make to you whether or not I was?"

He shrugged. "Just my big ego. You know. I don't like knowin' any woman I know as well as you isn't the least bit attracted to me."

She knew that wasn't true. She wanted to say, *See? See? You love me, or you wouldn't care*, but she said jerkily, "Well—you know now—I guess."

He turned his head and looked at her directly. He was smiling his mocking smile when he murmured, "Still shy of me, little Sara? Can't even admit you want me?"

She gasped. He didn't wait for an answer. "I'm sorry for dragging you into this tonight." His voice turned rough. "I knew I'd end up bashing Drew's face in. You shouldn't have seen it."

A couple of interesting things occurred to her; she decided to mention them. "You've told me, and I don't think you're angry. Are you?"

Slowly, he shook his head. "Not really. Just sick of it."

"You took quite a lot from him, until he said something nasty about me. I should be flattered, I suppose. My hero.''

He snorted derisively. "More like your moron! Lord help me—Sara, I don't have any sense. I don't have any ethics. I don't have any goals. Why do you even care?''

I love you. She didn't say it. She took a shaky breath. "It's not true that—" Before she could finish, they heard the front door open and footsteps on the flagstones.

Owen gave a quiet groan and dropped his head back on his arms. "Tell me that's not Drew.''

"It's Haddon.''

Owen didn't move. Sara went to meet his brother halfway.

He had a hat in one hand and her purse in the other. "Owen alive?''

"More or less, yes. I don't think he wants to be lectured.''

"Never lectured anybody in my life. Wouldn't know how.''

"Is Drew really all right?''

"Reckon he'll be wearing turtlenecks awhile. Elsewise, he'll do. Talked assault charges for a couple of minutes. Calmed down now, though. Knows if he'd been sober, Owen couldn't've pinned him.''

"Owen's still upset. He'll have a colorful face, and I don't think he'll be eating taffy for a few days, but I think he's all right.''

"This is his.''

She took the hat and purse and extended her palm when Haddon dangled a ring of keys in front of her. "Thanks. He was hunting them. . . . I'm sorry about your party.''

"Object *was* to get them together. Maybe now they've let off some steam they'll be able to talk like sane people.''

"You knew this would happen," Sara accused gently.

Haddon's shoulders lifted. "Wasn't surprised. If you'd been around in the old days, when Drew still lived here, you wouldn't've been surprised, either. 'Fact," he added, his eyes crinkling at their corners, "you probably would've known better than to accept Owen's invite. Tell him he's still welcome in what's left of my house."

Sara went back to the pickup. Owen hadn't moved, and she felt a stab of mother-hen worry again. *What is it with you?* he had asked. She could imagine what his expression would have been if she had replied simply, "I love you." She couldn't think of anything that would kill their strange friendship more quickly than that. Love meant ties and obligations. He was—at least he professed to be—a man who wanted no ties. He wanted love, but no ties. . . . His life had confused him so much that he didn't know what he wanted, and she was nearly as confused herself.

"Here." She dropped his hat on the hood.

"Have we been eighty-sixed?"

"Very kindly." She jingled the keys beside his ear. "Maybe I should drive."

He pushed up from the hood, drawing in another slow, deep breath. "It's a stick."

She handed him the keys. "Maybe you should drive." She went around the back of the pickup. He settled his hat comfortably, gingerly exploring his jaw. "Haddon says you're still welcome in what's left of his house," she said.

"What a guy."

She opened the passenger door and tossed Owen's vest onto the seat before she saw, highlighted by the dome light, the boxes in the pickup bed.

"Owen."

"No more, okay, Sara? Just—no more."

"Your grandfather's things are still here."

"Too bad." He was climbing into the cab.

She shut her door and reached for the smallest box. "I'll take them inside and ask Haddon to put them in the attic."

Owen groaned, rolled out of the cab, and slammed the door. "Sara!"

"Well, you don't want them at the shop! I'm not taking them home with me, and I'll bet anything you don't want to take them home with you. It's stupid not to leave them now. It won't take two minutes."

He snarled something under his breath and dragged the larger box over the side of the bed.

"You don't have to go," Sara said, coming around with the smaller box.

"You think I'll let you lug these while I sit and sulk in the truck?"

"I think it'd be a good thing if you and Drew didn't come face to face again."

"Don't you mean fist to face?" he asked with a ragged return of his satirical grin. "We'll leave them by the door. I promise to be good."

She expressed some doubt that he knew how. They argued about it quietly as they went up the steps.

The front part of the house was empty. Sara heard Donna and Haddon's voices coming from the kitchen and saw light shining beneath the door.

"Sounds like they're in there."

"Good." Owen started up the stairs.

"You said we would just leave them here!" Sara whispered after him.

"I lied." He glanced down at her. "Us *dastards* lie all the time. We'll stow them and silently steal away. With you along, I'm not so sure how silent we can be."

That remark made it impossible to grumble as she would have liked, while she trudged up the stairs behind him. They reached the second-floor landing and doubled back up a narrower, steeper flight of stairs.

The attic door was a skinny version of a normal door, set into the ceiling. Owen set his box on a step and pushed the door up into the black space beyond. He picked up the box and went on up, warning, "Careful, little Sara. I don't know where the light switch is."

She followed him slowly into the chilly darkness, stepping up onto the solid attic floor, puffing slightly from the unaccustomed exertion of climbing stairs.

A tiny, louvered window in the gable let the puniest rays shine in from the security light. Sara turned nearly a full 360 degrees but could see only vague, lumpy black shapes here and there. Nothing moved. She heard no sound.

"Owen," she said suspiciously, "what are you doing?"

Pseudo-maniacal laughter exploded behind her as two powerful arms wrapped around her from behind. The box of ledgers dropped with a thud, barely missing her toes. She would have shrieked if Owen had not growled softly, wickedly, against her ear, "This, little Sara. I'm doing this."

EIGHT

It was almost perfect, Sara thought afterward, as if they were doing a dance step they had practiced many times. She turned within his arms, slid her arms around his hard body, and lifted her face. The silverbelly hat bumped her forehead. He murmured an apology and loosened his hold long enough to remove the hat and sail it off into the darkness before he tipped her head back and kissed her.

It was not the kind of kiss Sara expected. It was nothing like Kevin's—demanding and wet. It was not even like Owen's crude, starving kiss that long-ago Halloween—that kiss had been hard and hurting, a staggering kiss that had commanded her submission.

He was gentle, almost hesitant, as if wary of his reception. His muscular, strong arms cradled her. His sensitive hands carefully molded her body to his.

His lips were warm and tasted faintly of coffee. She'd expected to feel a shy stirring of pleasure when they touched hers. Instead, her electrical system blew a fuse in a great shower of warm sparks. She caught her breath at the unexpected sensations that began down in the core of her body, hot and liquid, washing out toward him as his mouth caressed hers.

He murmured her name. He slanted his mouth and his lips gently nipped at hers until she relaxed, melting against him. She didn't have his experience, but she followed her loving instincts, returning the small nips of his mouth, digging her nails into his back through the cloth of his shirt under his coat, trying to get impossibly closer to him. The tip of his tongue flicked her lips, probing gently.

"Open your mouth," he breathed against it.

"Wha—?"

It was all he needed. Jubilantly, his tongue darted inside her, seductive and thrusting, teasing, tangling as his hesitancy evaporated. His lips bit tenderly at her mouth, sucking the kisses she offered. Those cunning hands found their way inside her jacket and pulled the satin shirttail out of her jeans, sliding over her bare back, drawing her closer into the warm, protective curve of his body.

"Oh, little Sara," he finally whispered, softly, into her hair. "I surely do like this blouse—*a lot!*"

She buried a feeble laugh in his collar, soaking up the familiar, male smell of him, feeling the warm, rough skin of his hands smooth sensually over her bare satin back. "Owen, *four years!*"

Four years wasted, was what she meant, four years when they might have kissed and shared and held each other. She didn't have to say that. He understood.

"Crime," he whispered in the darkness, tightening his arms. "So help me—the way you didn't even say good-bye—I didn't think you'd want to hear from me."

"Stupid." She burrowed closer to the vibrant warmth of his big body, sliding a hand between them, over his chest, to feel his heart beat beneath hard bone and muscle.

"Who's stupid? I'm not the one who saw me in the

Rim Shot with a blonde and was too put out to say fare-thee-well because of it.''

"Did you know I saw you?"

"Not till you told me the other day. I went home alone that night, honey, and I don't even remember her name."

"I told Robert to tell you I said good-bye."

"Robert," he answered testily, "said, 'Oh, by the way, Sara said so long.' "

"Well, I'm sorry, but you could have called me. You never called me."

He folded. "You're right. I am stupid." He nuzzled a kiss against her throat, sending warm goosebumps scrambling down over her breasts. "Mmmm, precious," he murmured approvingly. "Better than last time?"

"Last time?" she repeated muzzily.

"Halloween."

"Oh, yes. Much better."

"Good." His warm mouth lingered over hers again, brushing, teasing. "Good."

She whispered shakily, "Do you really not know where the light switch is?"

"I told you us dastards lie all the time." The cool tip of his tongue explored her ear, jerking a whimper of delight out of her.

"I never knew . . ."

"What? That a touch in your ear could make you feel good all over?"

"Y—yes. Owen—it's scary."

"Don't be scared, precious. I know how to be gentle."

I've had plenty of practice, he might as well have added, but she shoved that uncomfortable thought away. She kissed the swelling on his cheek, so gently, and he murmured insincerely, "Ow."

"Your poor face, all bruised and swollen. That's supposed to make it feel better."

"I know. I've got other bruises, too. They all need to feel better."

"Where?"

"All over. In amazing places."

"Sure," she said skeptically, and pushed back from him, nervous in this confusing, foreign territory.

His hands slid down and spread, pulling her pelvis firmly against his. "I have," he murmured pointedly into her ear, "some other swollen places, too. All needing to feel better."

He was immensely excited. His rigid body thrust against her, shocking a blast of heat through her. Her skin slid against the black satin shirt as he pulled her up against his chest. She suddenly wanted crazy things she had never even imagined. She wanted to slip her hands beneath the front of his jeans and explore him. She wanted their clothes to vaporize so her breasts could rub against his naked skin instead of the satin, so she could kiss her way down his body. She wanted him without thinking about the results, the pain that would come when he walked away from her as he had from all the others. She went up on her toes to press her body closer to his, exploring the skin of his neck with her mouth as her hands smoothed the hard muscles of his back.

His fingers squirmed their way to the buttons on the satin blouse as he gave a groan of approval. On the small, satin-covered rounds, his fingers were deft and sure and seemed too practiced. She felt chilled suddenly, and whispered shakily, "Wait. Owen. Wait."

"Wait?" His voice was taut, even rougher than usual. "What are we waiting for, precious? Don't you know what you do to me? I feel like an oil well on fire. I want you," he said huskily. "I want you wrapped warm and tight around me." His hands tormented her breasts, gentle but stroking relentlessly through smooth fabric. His touch made her weak. Her soft, responding moan excited him.

"*Yes,*" he whispered sharply. His lips explored the hollow of her throat while his thumbs teased, brushed. "Sara, I can give you so much pleasure—you won't believe it. You'll moan for me, baby."

She had always thought *baby* sounded crude and somehow demanding but now, breathed gently from his lips, the word sounded natural and loving. She opened her mouth to say so, but a sound from below stopped her.

"Owen," she murmured against his whiskery jaw, "someone's coming up."

"Your imagination."

The sounds of booted feet on the treads were quite plain. She gave a laugh. "I don't think so."

"It's the sound of your heart beating longingly for me."

She smothered another laugh. "No, I think—"

"Who in tarnation's in the attic? Matthew, is that you up in the attic?" Haddon's voice was louder and more threatening than Sara had ever heard it. She pulled back from Owen and began shoving her blouse back into her jeans. Owen heaved a large, ostentatious sigh.

"No," he said loudly, "it's not Matthew. Stop caterwauling, will you? People are trying to sleep, and read, and whatnot."

"Owen?" Haddon sounded dismayed. "Thought you'd gone home. What the blazes are you doin' up there in the dark?"

"I couldn't find the light switch," Owen replied, making Sara give him a poke in the ribs with her knuckles for his lie. He snickered and his hands reached for her. She started to retreat, but his fingers were simply doing up the two silk-wrapped buttons he'd had time to free from their slots. "We brought some boxes of Granddad's stuff up here. You don't object, do you?"

Haddon had stopped, Sara figured, on the landing. "Who's we?"

Owen finished the last button, gave Sara's stomach a friendly rub with the back of his hand, and turned away into the shadows.

"Oh, Julia Roberts, Kathleen Turner, and Madonna dropped by. They'd heard about your attic and wanted a tour, and you know me—always happy to oblige a lady."

Sara heard Haddon make an exasperated noise and start up the narrow stairs. She smoothed her hair. Her lipstick was long gone, but she wiped her mouth in case of a lingering smear.

"It's actually just me," she said, going down the steps, hoping she didn't look as caught-in-the-jam-jar as she felt. "We lugged up some old ledgers and so on from the shop. You ought to take a look at them sometime. Owen found an interesting letter, did he tell you?"

Haddon stopped just above the landing, looking up at her. The suspicion in his eyes lasted only a moment; she felt more guilty than ever, because she could read his thoughts. It was only Sara. If it had been anyone else, he'd have figured Owen had been up to no good in there, but since it was Sara . . .

"What kind of letter?"

"From George Phippen. Remember, Granddad used to say he'd made a hat for him?" Owen's voice came hollowly from above. "It's not here, though. I've got it at th—" The sentence finished with a solid thud, punctuated by a word Sara hoped the kids couldn't hear. A moment later, he came down the stairs behind her, limping slightly, rubbing his thigh, his retrieved hat in his other hand.

He expanded on the subject of the artist's letter as

they descended. By the time they went out the front door, Sara was sure Haddon had forgotten to wonder about their being in the attic.

Owen had to have the last word. Halfway down the sloped lawn, he called back facetiously, "Thanks for a really special evening, Had'n."

Haddon growled and closed the front door rather loudly, making Owen grin.

"Was that necessary?" Sara inquired.

"Yes."

They climbed into Owen's pickup, and he started the engine as Sara buckled up. She was shivering, partly, she thought, from being kissed half to death in the attic.

"I can't wait until there's some heat!"

"Well, guess I forgot to mention," Owen said, negotiating the drive, "the blower motor went out in this yesterday. Haven't had a chance to replace it. Sorry."

She hugged herself. "I'm freezing!"

"Scoot over here."

"I want a seat belt."

He rummaged under his vest and produced a belt. "Voilà."

She slowly turned and looked at him. A ton of bricks did not have to fall on Sara Dugan. Before he could stop her, she shot out a hand and flipped the blower switch to high.

Nothing happened.

"I *told* you," Owen said righteously. "Dang, what a suspicious mind!"

"Maybe I figured a man who couldn't f-find a light, switch t-twice in a row couldn't f-find a heater switch, either!"

He laughed and snaked a hand over to the buckle of her seat belt. "Come on. Scoot over. Put my vest over you and cinch up. Do it, darlin'," he finished gently. "You'll be numb by the time I get you home if you don't."

She stared at him through the darkness for a long moment. It was not that she didn't trust him. She didn't trust herself. She had learned a surprising something about herself back in Haddon's attic. Owen could have anything he wanted from her. Anything.

She slid across the seat into the comforting circle of his arm.

She buckled up, wrapped his down vest around her, and allowed him to pull her against his shoulder. It was incredibly comfortable. The wool of his coat scrubbed her cheek pleasantly. She couldn't decide what to do with her right hand, which was cold. He solved that by saying, "'Warm your hand inside my coat."

She tucked her fingers between the buttons, curling them against the warmth of his flat belly.

They rode in comfortable silence, but Sara's mind noisily mulled over the hectic afternoon, everything from the outspoken opinions of Matthew to the brawl. It was inevitable that she would come around to the minutes spent in the attic. "Do you think . . ."

"Hardly ever. Ask anybody."

"Stop it." She was quiet then, because what she had been going to say suddenly sounded silly.

"Do I think what?" He stroked her cheek with one finger.

"Do you think Haddon believed we were doing what we said we were doing in the attic?"

"Who cares?"

"I do."

He was silent for a time, his shoulder moving beneath her cheek with each breath he took. " 'Course you do. Sorry. Most of my experience has been with women who didn't care who was looking on." He gave a sigh. "We *were* doing what we said we were doing, you know, stowing Granddad's stuff. I don't know what Haddon thought, honey. I guarantee, if he thought we were playing slap and tickle up there, it'd be my fault and my responsibility, not yours.''

"You didn't twist my arm."

"I like to save something for the second date. . . . Don't worry about it. Whatever Haddon thinks, he's not gonna say anything to anybody about it, one way or another. You won't be shamed by it."

"I wouldn't be ashamed of it—of you, if that's what you mean," she said indignantly. "I'm just not—''

"Used to it," he finished obligingly. "How many men have you kissed, Sara?"

"How many *men* have I kissed?"

"I asked you first." He gave her shoulders a mildly threatening squeeze. "How many?"

"That's an embarrassing question!"

"Best get it over with quick-like, then."

"My father, and my brother—''

"I meant *men*, little Sara."

"My manly father and brother would be insulted."

"Your father's past caring, and Robert ought to be insulted now and then, on general principles. How many, Sara?"

"Why do you want to know?"

"Because I'm a nosy S.O.B. with no manners. How many, little Sara?"

She thought about sitting up and squirming away from him. She was reasonably warm now, and they were halfway home.

It was too much trouble.

"Owen—''

"I'll help. Kevin. That's one."

"Very good—you got his name right on the first try."

"Miracles happen. Who else?"

"You . . ."

"And?"

"Just . . . you."

He let up on the accelerator and she could feel him looking down at the top of her head. "Sara Dugan," he said, "are you suffering from amnesia?"

"Hmm-mmm," she murmured into his coat.

"You mean I was the first man to kiss you?"

"Mmm-hmmm."

"Oh, Sara . . . forgive me for the way I did it."

She said sleepily, "Already did a long time ago."

He could feel her relax then, vulnerable and trusting. He sat there with his breath stuck in his chest, his thoughts banging around like a bunch of mad bees in a bottle. It seemed incredible. . . . She had already turned *eighteen*. It had been a young eighteen, though. He had known her to have a few boy friends, but no boyfriend. He shook his head, but it didn't clear. It had simply never occurred to him that one reason she had been so unresponsive to him that first time was that she hadn't known how to respond. All the women dumb Devil Dixon had known up until then seemed to have been born possessing certain arts. Kissing was one of them.

Even tonight, he thought now, she had not been skilled, but she had followed his lead and given him back such sweetness from her heart that her inexperience hadn't mattered, hadn't even registered until now. He didn't know whether to think better or worse of Kevin for what Sara had obviously not learned from him.

He hit a red light at the intersection where the Beeline met 260. He had to take his arm from around Sara in order to shift down. It roused her enough that she shifted her head and burrowed her hand farther inside his coat.

"Warm enough?" he asked.

She nodded sleepily. She whispered something and seemed to sink back into her doze. He sat there, staring through the intersection, while the light turned green and back to red and green again. If a car hadn't come up behind and honked on the second change, who knew how long he might have sat there?

Sara didn't go back to sleep, but she pretended to. Owen remained slightly rigid with shock and—fear?—until they were home. He didn't even replace his arm around her.

She hadn't been conscious of deciding the time was right. She wasn't even sure the time *had* been right. She had opened her mouth and the words had slid out, and there was no pulling them back now, so she relaxed against him, with her heart bruising her breastbone and her hand clenched into a tight, fearful fist against his abdomen until she knew by the feel of the tilt of the truck that they were in the driveway.

"Sara, wake up."

She took a deep breath and sat up, stretching.

"The house's dark," Owen said in an odd, tight voice. "I don't see Robert's truck."

"Mmm. He probably had another emergency call." She disengaged herself from Owen's vest and popped the seat belt free. "Good, that means I can go right to bed without having to make conversation until the wee hours."

Owen turned off the engine. "I'll walk you to the door."

"No, thanks. Just keep the headlights on the door until I get in, please?"

Her hands trembled as she fumbled for her purse, but he wouldn't be able tell in the darkness.

He didn't answer, and she quit fussing to look at his face. He was watching her. He watched her until she gave up and reached for the door handle, then his hand came out and caught her left forearm in a firm grip.

"Sara." His voice still sounded strange, but it was gentle. He sounded mildly stymied. "Do you remember my asking if you were warm enough a few minutes ago?"

"Yes," she said calmly. "At the light."

"Yeah. And were you awake enough to know what you said to me after that? 'Cause I wasn't sure I heard you right. Maybe I didn't hear you right. I probably didn't hear you right."

"Yes," she said, realizing with some awe that, of the two of them, she was in much better control at the moment. "I know what I said, Owen. I said, 'I love you.' Was that what you thought?"

He cleared his throat and shifted his body to partially face hers. "Yes," he said very slowly.

I thought you said an atomic bomb had dropped on my house.

Yes, that's what I said.

Ah. I thought that's what you said.

"Would you like a cup of coffee or hot chocolate, or something?" she offered.

"No," he replied gruffly, "I don't want coffee or hot chocolate, or anything."

"Well, thanks for bringing me home. Good night, then." She leaned to him, quickly, and carefully put a kiss among the late-night whiskers on his bruised jaw. It only made his hand tighten on her arm until it was almost painful.

"Sara?"

It was so rare to be the one not flustered or embarrassed or shocked by what the other had said. She said gently, "It's nothing new, you know. I've loved you for years. I told you for a change, that's all. Don't let it blow a circuit."

When she reached for the door again, he gave her arm a little jerk.

"Sara," he said with an obvious effort to be unruffled, "you can't love me."

"Too bad. I do."

"Sara—"

"I wish you would de-clamp my arm. My fingers are going to sleep."

He looked down at his hand and, with sudden awareness, released her as if she had sprouted razors.

"Sara, I'm not kidding. You can't—I'm not—" He stopped and took a deep breath. "You know me. I'm not the man for you."

She held on to her heart, kept it from sinking much beyond her stomach. "I think I should be allowed to decide that."

He shook his head. "No. You can't. There're things you don't know about me. What you do know should tell you not to trust me any more than a weasel in a chicken coop. . . . You mean a lot to me, you know you do, but you said yourself that you had a crush on me, and that's all this is. You deserve a man who'll be there when you need him, not off gallivanting with some other woman. You deserve a man you can depend on, who'll give you a nice, vine-covered cottage and a bunch of kids, and a couple of cats, and some roses in the yard. . . . All you'd ever get from me is a world of hurt, and you know it."

The awful thing was, she was afraid he was right about the last part. She said serenely, "Cats are snobs, and kids are not all they're cracked up to be. You said *yourself* that I know more about you than anybody. I don't say I necessarily like it all, but I love you anyway. It isn't a crush. That phased out a long time ago and left something a lot more permanent behind. And you know something? When it comes to the things that matter to you, you're as dependable as any man on earth. Anyway," she said, successfully grabbing the door handle this time, "I just said I love you, I didn't ask you to marry me or build me a vine-covered cottage. If it bothers you so much, I won't say it again. I'll see you in the morning."

"Sara—I—don't want you to stumble over me and get hurt!"

"Then don't trip me."

The cab was silent for a moment.

"What?"

"I said," she repeated very gently, "don't trip me."

She slipped out the door without looking back at him and went up the steps in the white glare of the head-lights. She unlocked the front door and paused inside to wave at him. He flicked the brights on and off, then backed down the drive. She could hear the truck purr down the quiet residential street as she shot the dead-bolt lock behind her.

Who would think a simple thing like an *I love you* would send Devil Dixon into such a tailspin? She smiled wistfully as she went through the house, turning on lights, remembering the shock that had filled him to overflowing. It was probably good for him. It was probably something he hadn't heard much.

No, he hadn't heard it much, Owen thought grimly as he navigated the familiar dark roads toward his own house. Not since Mel Page. Not since she'd told him how she loved him, meanwhile busily getting pregnant by some other jerk.

This was his own fault. He'd flirted with and harassed and dreamed about Sara all week long, then tonight . . . he'd lost it. Sara in the dark in the attic had been too good to pass up. He felt about Sara as he had never felt about any other woman, even Mel. Wanting her soft curves and minty taste, honey hair and carnation smell were only part of it. He wanted her sense of humor and her quick mind that seemed able to dance and twist with his. He wanted her sense of integrity, her trust, her friendship, her . . . love.

That didn't change the fact that he had meant every word he'd said to her. He wasn't the man for her. He was not the man for any woman.

Was he?

No, but . . .

Was he?

No.

Clouds moved in the next morning on wind that blew cold, as if snow lay behind it. Sara reached the shop ahead of Owen and was standing on the steps, shivering again, when he pulled up.

He got out of his truck and came up, looking at her curiously, she thought. His right cheek was swollen and discolored. His granite eyes looked odd in the peculiar, clouded light, wicked and hard and cold as the wind.

She said, " 'Morning."

" 'Mornin'."

He inserted the key in the lock and went in ahead of her. "Brrrr!" she said, coming out of the tunnel into the shop.

He opened the stove.

Sara said, "Another storm coming in."

Owen silently shoved kindling into the stove.

"We could use some more rain, but I wish it wouldn't snow."

He tossed a burning match into the stove strategically. Little crackles began emanating from it. He shrugged out of his coat.

"I'll finish up the statements," Sara said, "unless you have something else you want me to do first?"

He glanced at her and said, "No. Yes."

"That's decisive."

He threw his coat at the rack in the corner and it actually caught a hook. "I want you to do statements today, yes," he said, "but first I want to say something to you."

She took one look at the expression in his eyes, at the small lines bracketing his mouth, and pulled her own coat closer around her. "I don't think so."

He came around the counter, blocking her way into the back room.

"Owen," she said reasonably, "you're mad. I don't think you should make any declarations while you're mad."

"I'm not mad." His expression eased. "Well, if I am, it's me I'm mad at." He folded his arms across his middle and leaned a shoulder against the doorjamb. "You gotta understand this, Sara. I meant what I said last night."

"I know."

His eyes searched her face carefully. "Did you mean what you said last night?"

"Yes."

"Still mean it this morning?"

"Oh, yes."

He nodded slightly, as if saying *I was afraid of that.* "Well, then, here's the way it's got to be. You know I can still use your help until Maddox comes. If you want to work here through the rest of next week, you're welcome. But you've got to agree we'll keep our hands off each other, and no suggestive remarks, and no nonsense. I'm your employer, you're my employee, and that's all."

Sara had not expected this. She stared at him, trying to see inside the workings of his mind, to understand exactly where he was headed. She must have looked extremely distressed, she thought, or inordinately feeble-minded, because his expression gentled and he lowered his voice slightly.

"Sara, we've been friends a long time. There've been time gaps, but we've always come back together, like we did the day you walked in here after this job. Outside of Haddon, you're the only one I've ever really been able to depend on. I don't want to risk losing that. I'm not willing to trade being friends with you for

. . ." He left that hanging, suddenly uncharacteristically awkward.

"A couple of nights in the sack?" she finished for him with a sickening choke in her throat.

"Delicately put," he agreed dryly. "It couldn't be more than that. So, only thing I know to do is make sure something like last night doesn't happen again. Now, it means enough to me that I *can* keep my hands to myself. If you can live with that, then we'll get on with it. If you can't, you'd better hunt another job."

Well. Gentled expression and lowered voice notwithstanding, that had been a nasty zinger.

"You mean until after Mr. Maddox has gone?"

"No—I mean forever."

Oh, God. Oh, God, no. This isn't the way it's supposed to turn out.

"Do you think that will make me stop loving you? Or you me?"

He flinched as if he'd been jabbed with a needle. It took him a moment to speak. Then his voice was infuriatingly kind. "I'm sorry, Sara . . . I don't love you. Except, maybe, the way I'd love a little sister if I had one."

"Excuse me? Do I understand that you would kiss a little sister the way you kissed me last night?"

It made him angry. She wasn't sure why, but the granite in his eyes shattered into bits of flat, cloudy anger. "Come on, don't be so naive! I'm a man! Don't you know that just because a woman's particular chemistry excites a man, it doesn't mean he's in love with her?"

They stared wrathfully at each other until Owen relented, blowing out a sharp sigh. "Sara, this is to keep our friendship together!"

"Fine." She pushed past him into the back room.

She went to the desk and began rummaging blindly through the papers she had left on top. She heard Owen come in after her and knew he stood close behind her, watching for a minute or so.

"Sara, are you ticked off at me?"

She swung around. She had not been little Sara since sometime last night, she realized. After having had the reasonable desire to be called something less patronizing all last week, she now had the unreasonable desire to be little Sara again. She looked at Owen's face and found a sort of squinty amusement in his eyes as he watched her.

"No, I'm not," she answered flatly. "I'm sure you'll think this is stupid, but what I'm actually ticked off at is *love*."

His dark eyebrows climbed into their wicked, satiric arcs.

"I mean—I wish love were—bigger, more tangible. Like a—a gorilla or a saguaro! I want to be able to pick it up and shove it in your face and say, 'There, that's what it looks like! Recognize it, now?' You love me, Owen, I know you do! But you don't see it, and"—her voice dwindled—"if you don't believe it, then we're no better off than if you didn't love me. . . . So. You want friendship? I've given you friendship for years. I guess I can do it some more. Fine. That's all. There's lots of work to do, so let's get to work."

He watched her fuss with the papers. He watched while she settled in the big leather chair, huddled in her coat, and bent over the work with a pencil clutched so tightly that her fingers ached. What was he waiting for anyway? Tears? A nervous breakdown? Levitation?

He said quietly, "There'll be somebody else—somebody who'll treat you right."

"Yes," she agreed tonelessly, "I'm sure there will be. And I, of course, will be eternally grateful for your having made me wait for him."

"Right," he agreed, and he sounded odd as he turned away.

"Hey, how's your face?"

"What?"

"Your *face*. How's your face? That stuff that conceals what passes for your brain? It looks uncomfortable. Does it hurt?"

"Only when I laugh."

He went back to the stove and stood there staring at the front of it, shaking all over.

It wasn't what he wanted. It wasn't even close.

NINE

Having typed all the statements and a history of the shop, and put them, together with a clear photocopy of the *Horse Source* article, in a professional-looking presentation package to be given to Mr. Maddox upon his arrival, Sara turned her attention to other things.

On Tuesday, after doing her paper chores, she dragged Robert's big industrial vacuum in—Owen didn't offer to help—and attacked the corners and crannies of the shop. She climbed a stepladder and, using the vacuum's long extension hose, sucked the cobwebs from the open rafters. She moved antiques and crawled on the floor until her knees ached. She knew the noise frayed Owen's nerves, but he didn't say much about it. He didn't say much about anything, in fact, and they were quite careful to keep away from each other.

On Wednesday, Sara met Danielle.

She was wearing old clothes again that morning, and had brought lemon oil and rags to polish the furnishings.

"A janitor service comes in, you know," Owen objected, coming exasperatedly out of yesterday's patient, quiet shell. "I'm not paying you maid's wages.

166

There're other things you could be doing. Answering yesterday's mail, for one.''

"A maid probably makes more than you're paying me. The mail is done.'' She nodded to where she had put envelopes by the cash register. "Janitor services swipe a feather duster around and vacuum some. They don't have time for much else. They certainly don't lemon-oil antiques.''

"So what? Everything's clean—especially after yesterday—my ears still ring from that dad-ratted monstrosity you lugged in here! If Maddox buys the place, he's not buying the furniture.''

"Wrong!'' Sara goaded. "It may not be your hat business he's after, but you're selling the building's image. The furnishings are part of it. What you want is for everything to look so good his mind will be tricked into believing it's the charm of the *building* that appeals to him. It's like when you sell a home; the idea is for even the closets to be clean and organized so that a prospective buyer pokes around and thinks, 'My, this house holds an awful lot of stuff and looks so neat while it does it, too.' Same principle.''

"You've sold a lot of homes, have you?'' Owen asked heavily, knowing she presently lived in the house in which she'd grown up.

"Didn't I mention?'' She smiled sweetly. "Kevin was a real estate agent. His whole family's in real estate. I learned a lot from Kevin.''

He stared at her, then his eyes dropped down to her mouth and he grinned. Then he laughed, a snickering, enjoying kind of laugh. It didn't last long, then he just looked irritated. "Yeah. Well, there're still other things I'd rather you'd do, since you're on my payroll. Leave this cosmetic stuff until Friday if there's time.''

"No,'' Sara said firmly, making his eyebrows wing up arrogantly. "This stuff''—she waved an oil-soaked rag at him—"smells.''

"Got that right, lady."

"If I leave this until Friday, the whole place will reek of oil. If I do it now, by Friday the oil will have soaked in, the odor will have dissipated, and even if he notices what we've done, it won't wallop him in the face when he walks in. He'll just get that lovely, furry, steamy smell."

"Lovely, furry—a lot of folks wrinkle their noses at the smell."

"Why do you think I've come here all these years?"

"I thought it was to moon over me," he said wickedly.

She couldn't deny that without telling a bald-faced lie. She sniffed, shook a rag out, and began polishing the dickens out of a mirror frame.

By noon, the shop looked better than she had ever seen it. Even Owen reluctantly admitted that it looked "all right" as he took a hat into the back room.

He hadn't been at the flanging bag more than two minutes when the harness brasses jingled. Sara, giving the glass over the Duke Hat a final spray of glass cleaner, didn't have to look in the mirror to see Beauty coming down the tunnel into the shop.

Beauty had rich, dark auburn hair, so Sara never even guessed. She was tall and curvy, in tight jeans, a snug denim jacket, and spike-heeled boots to her knees. Dangly gold hoops flirted from her ears. Her eye shadow was green.

"Hi!" the cinnamon-haired witch chirped. "You must be Sara."

"I must be," Sara agreed, thinking that it was something Owen might have said. "What can I help you with?"

Beauty stared thoughtfully for a moment, her green eyes scaling with interest over Sara's baggy old sweater and lemon-oily jeans. "I'm Danielle Williams."

Sara knew her mouth dropped open slightly. "Oh," she said cleverly.

"I've heard a lot about you." The green eyes took in Sara's knotted hair and smudged, makeup-free face. A small smirk formed on her mouth as she plainly decided she had nothing to fear from Sara. "Owen talks about you all the time."

Does he?

"He's told me about you, too." *Barely,* Sara added silently. "I thought you were a blonde."

"I am sometimes." Danielle grinned engagingly. "Is Owen in back?"

"Yes," Sara said. "I'll get him."

"Don't bother. I know the way."

"Right." Sara watched Danielle spike-heel her way around the counter and into the back room. She heard Owen say "Hey" in a friendly way, then things were quiet; not even the steam pot hissed.

Sara stood motionless, terminal numbness creeping over her.

Danielle wasn't right; she wasn't right at all. She didn't fit the profile. Owen liked sophisticated blondes, not perky, capricious redheads. Mel Page had been willowy and flaxen-haired, much like Drew's Marcy.

It was not uncommon, she had heard, for a man to fall in love with and marry someone utterly different than his "type." Danielle was surely that. What if Owen actually loved that redhead? Why shouldn't he love that redhead? He and Sara were *just friends,* after all. He was free to love a redheaded woman, or even a bald-headed woman, if he wanted to. Sara wasn't his type, either, yet she was convinced Owen was in love with her. . . .

Sara brought her irresponsible, bitter thoughts to a skidding halt and finished polishing the Duke Hat's case. If her ears strained to hear the smallest sound from the back room, it was only out of curiosity. If, as she turned back to the counter, her eyes strayed toward the doorway to the back room, it was only from sisterly concern. If what she saw froze her into immobility and sent real pain knifing through her chest, it was what she deserved for spying.

Owen's hands were shoved deeply into the front pockets of his Levi's, as if he'd been caught slightly off guard, and Danielle's were rubbing pleasurably across the denim that lay over his—in Sara's opinion—very fine, tight backside. You couldn't have slid a gum wrapper between their bodies, and their mouths were joined together in the widest, deepest kiss Sara had ever seen off a movie screen.

She didn't know how long she would have stood there, gazing, peeping, if she hadn't heard a sound of bliss from Danielle and a small growl in Owen's throat. She jerked her eyes away and went behind the counter, where she stood with her fingers strangling the bottle of glass cleaner, staring at the register. She stood that way, thinking *He's entitled, he's a free man, and if he's happy, I am happy* over and over, as if that would make her believe it. What seemed like hours—but was actually only seconds—later, she heard Danielle say, "I have to go."

"That's a pity," Owen said.

There were indistinguishable murmurs and Danielle giggled, then Sara heard her ask, "Will you take me out tonight?"

"Nope. Got other plans, but I'll call you in a day or two. You . . . simmer on the back burner for me, will you?"

Danielle laughed, a soft, knowing laugh that turned Sara's already sluggish blood to tapioca, and a moment later, she came out through the shop.

"Nice to meet you, Sara," she said softly, while her catty green eyes danced.

Sara couldn't even summon up a polite reply. She

watched Danielle's tightly encased hips swivel into the tunnel and, once the door had closed and the harness brasses had shut up, she forced her hands open and put the cleaner and rag on the counter.

Owen was standing in the doorway when she turned. His shoulder was propped against the jamb, his arms folded, his hat pushed forward at a cocky angle, and there was a smug smirk on his mouth.

The smirk faded when he saw her face. He looked at her for a moment, motionless, then said, "She kissed *me*."

Sara swallowed a couple of times and managed to shrug a shoulder. "Who cares?"

His eyebrows rose slightly. "You do, by the look of you. You were watchin' us."

How did you know, when your eyes were closed to the rest of the world? . . . "I didn't mean to pry, but the door was open. I hope you're all right."

His granite eyes suddenly questioned and his dark slashes of brows rose up still more. "Some reason I shouldn't be?"

"I was afraid she might have hurt you, the way she had your arm twisted, that way."

"I get it," he said amiably. "I did try to tell you, Sara."

She took a deep breath, letting it out slowly, shakily. "Yes. You did. I didn't believe you. I guess I thought that, in your heart, you actually lov—loved me so much you couldn't care for anyone else. Wrong again." She knew she could not trust her voice much longer. She slid the glass cleaner under the counter and got her purse and jacket. "I think I'll go home now. I feel a little sick."

"Sara." There was a gruff and I-told-you-so sound to his voice.

As she slid into her jacket, she said, "I won't be

in until ten tomorrow. I have a job interview in the morning.''

She waited for his reaction. *A job interview!* he should say. *A job interview! No! No! Not that! Don't leave me, Sara!*

"Fine," Owen said, pushing away from the door-jamb and turning to go into the back. "Good luck."

"Then Friday will be my last day."

He paused, turning, sending another questioning gray look at her. "Are you sure? There's work for you. I'd thought once Maddox had been and gone, I'd start teaching you some. I thought that's what you wanted."

Sara paused in the mouth of the tunnel, and her voice sounded strained. "No thanks. I've changed my mind about that. I think you've already taught me as much as I can stand."

Sara wore a tailored blue suit, madras plaid shirt, neat navy tie, and navy heels on Thursday morning. Her hair, in its neat twist with its neat wisps, had the "glued on hair by hair" look she was famous for.

"My, my," Owen said when she walked in out of the chilly morning promptly at ten. "Don't we look snazzy?"

She eyed the yellowing bruise on his jaw. "One of us does."

"Get the job?"

"I don't know yet."

"Who'd you interview with?"

"Spencer Northfield."

"Northfield. The real estate agent?"

"Right."

"Well, hey. All that real estate knowledge you have should come in right handy."

Then he grinned, and she felt like slapping his face, but that would have involved touching him. By decree, touching was out.

"I thought so," she said pleasantly. "I meant to change before coming in, but I ran late. Shall I go do it? What do you plan for me to do today?"

"You mean I'm actually allowed to plan something? You're not gonna bring in a team of Belgians and plow up the back forty? Or start building an interstate through the bathroom?"

"I'll go home and change," she said stuffily. "It shouldn't take me more than twenty minutes."

He picked up a brass-studded leather hatband, put it on a just-finished hat, and squinted at it critically. "Don't bother, little Sara. This isn't a dirty job, you know. Coveralls and hip boots aren't necessary."

"Really?" She let the word slide over her shoulder as she went into the back room. "Some kind of boots are practically mandatory, considering what has to be waded through around here."

He laughed.

It was a nice sound, she thought as she slid her sleekly hosed knees under Benjamin's desk. And at least she was little Sara again.

The day worked out strangely, Sara thought later, as if cords had been gathered by a large, skillful hand and woven together in an unexpected, twisted pattern. If Sara hadn't told Owen she loved him, he wouldn't have retreated behind his wall of friendship, and if he hadn't done that, making working with him uncomfortable, she would have given no thought to finding another job until he had officially terminated her. If she hadn't gone on the job interview that morning, she would have come in at her usual time and gone home at noon. If she'd gone home at noon, she wouldn't have been there when Bentin Maddox walked in half a day early, surprise, surprise, and she wouldn't have wrecked her last decent pair of hose.

Bentin Maddox was a big man, taller and brawnier

than Owen, the type to run to paunch in his old age if he wasn't careful, while Owen, Sara thought with a certain amount of pride, would grow leaner, thinner, and whipcord tough like his grandfather. Maddox was still trim, though, and a Western-yoked black suit with the faintest hint of a pinstripe lay elegantly across his broad shoulders. Custom tailored and expensive, right down to his red silk tie, Sara thought as he introduced himself, but what else would you expect from a man whose family owned a chain of Western clothing stores?

He had one of those square jaws that heroes were supposed to have and a pair of thick-lashed, slightly slanted eyes like twin magic amulets.

"It's a pleasure to meet you," he said, shaking Owen's hand. "I've admired your hats many times."

Owen allowed his eyes to skim over the other man's carefully styled, sandy hair. "Why aren't you wearing one, then?"

Maddox grinned amiably. "And muss my hair? I didn't want to risk wearing my Stetson in here."

"Oh, we don't burn 'em anymore. We just stomp on 'em a little and throw them out in the rain. A man could do worse than wear a John B."

"That he could." Maddox surveyed Owen's discolored jaw and murmured, "Mule?"

"A little family squabble."

"Ah," Maddox said sympathetically. "I have six brothers and sisters, myself. Say no more." He turned his twinkling eyes on Sara. "Miss—Dugan, was it?"

"Sara, please."

"Sara, what an enhancement you are to the Dixon Hat Company." He cocked an eyebrow at Owen. "I don't suppose she comes with the facility."

Owen, Sara saw, was tempted to make an off-color reply, but he only grinned lazily. "Oh, Sara's a mighty independent young lady. No tellin'."

"Business must be good if you need an assistant."

"Can't complain. She's my bookkeeper, more or less. I'm not much on paperwork."

"I don't blame you." Maddox glanced appraisingly at Sara. "Not a bit."

Irritated at their talking past her, she said, "We didn't expect you until tomorrow, Mr. Maddox."

"When you know me better," he replied in a tone that insinuated she would, indeed, get to know him *much* better, "you'll learn surprise inspections are among my favorite things. You never know what they'll turn up. Ask my employees. Why don't you call me Ben? 'Mr. Maddox' is toxic, and my given name sounds like twisted metal." He grinned, trailing his eyes down along Sara's throat until she felt as if he'd touched her with chilled fingers. Unconsciously, she moved a little nearer to Owen for protection.

For about two seconds, Owen thought about punching Bentin Maddox in the nose for the look in his eyes, then sanity returned and he simply put one hand on Sara's shoulder in a way that could be friendly or brotherly—or possessive. He gave it a reassuring squeeze and rub, then dropped his hand away. "How about a cup of coffee?"

"I wouldn't say no. Charming old potbelly. Hardly adequate as a heat source, though."

"It takes the edge off." Owen fetched a mug and poured steaming, strong coffee from the pot. "There's no central heating, if that's what you're asking."

Maddox accepted the coffee as his unusual amulet eyes wandered among the clean, open beams. "I wasn't, but I'm not surprised. I understand the building is fifty years old."

"Part's older than that. A hunter's cabin was here when my grandfather bought the property. He added to it."

"Which is the oldest part?"

"The back room was the cabin. Take a look, if you'd like."

"I'd like."

There was nothing wrong with the words. Maddox's eyes settled on Sara as he said them, and it was all she could do not to shiver under their touch. Owen saw it, too. She saw his mouth tighten as he led Maddox into the back room. That was interesting. Could Owen be jealous? Owen could *not* be jealous, because they were Just Friends. He had said so. Anyway, he was the one who had said another man would come along for her. She studied Bentin Maddox's broad back before it disappeared into the back room. Could he be Mr. Right?

No.

As Maddox explored the shop's interior under Owen's watchful eye, Sara busied herself. While they were in the back room, she sorted through the morning's mail. When they came out into the shop, Maddox's blue eyes probing and scraping over everything, including Sara, she went back to the pigeonhole desk and disposed of the correspondence, trying to rid herself of the feeling she'd been touched by something unpleasant. When Owen called to say they were going outside, she went back to the front counter and played storekeeper.

They were outdoors for a long time. She could see them through the side window as they walked over the property. There was much pointing and talking, then sprinkles began and they came inside. Sara knew enough now to look into the mirror and watch Owen come in through the tunnel. He was grinning, but her impression was that the grin was at something in their conversation, not at any wonderful offer Maddox may have made for the shop. She questioned him with a look, but he shook his head.

"Damp up here," Maddox said.

"We need it." Owen headed for the coffee and poured

them each a cup. "Last thing in this world we want is another dry spell and a fire like the Dude Fire."

"That was terrible. I haven't been up into the area, but I saw it on the news, of course. Six firefighters killed, wasn't it?"

"Yeah. Sixty-odd homes burned."

"I understand it burned the Zane Grey cabin."

"That's right. Funny. It looks as though, if the cabin'd sat fifty feet in the right direction, it wouldn't have burned. The Dude was real selective."

"I understand they're going to rebuild it."

Owen shrugged. "Maybe. Last I heard, they hadn't raised enough money. I hear the owner's decided to sell the land."

"I'd like to go up there," Maddox said. "I hadn't seen the cabin since I was a kid. I'd like to see—"

The phone rang and Owen answered it. A moment later, he was heading for the back room to the files, and Sara carefully hung up the receiver after he'd picked up the phone at the pigeonhole desk.

Then nothing but the sales counter stood between her and Maddox.

He leaned one elbow on the high counter and sipped his coffee. "You," he observed softly, "are a quiet young lady."

She couldn't meet those peculiar amulet eyes. She fiddled with the hatband Owen had been working on before Maddox's arrival and said, "I think Owen's perfectly able to conduct his business without my interference."

"Zane Grey's cabin isn't business. Owen tells me you've lived here most of your life. You can probably tell me more about it. Why don't you?"

She forced her eyes to meet his for a moment. "I've been away for several years. I only know what I saw on the news." She heard Owen hang up the phone. "If you want more information, go up to Kohl's Ranch and

ask around. They can probably tell you more than anyone. Excuse me.''

She felt Maddox's eyes on her back as she passed
Owen, going into the back room. She dove into the
bookkeeping as if it were her life's dream.

On the alert, she popped out of the chair and spun
around to face the door when she heard boots on the
pine floor there. It was only Owen, who grinned, but
not unsympathetically.

''Jumpy, aren't you?''

''I thought—''

''I was Maddox?''

''Shhh!''

''He went out to his car for a copy of their new mail-
order catalog. I was wonderin' who you're hidin' from
back here, me or him.''

She lowered her voice and, in a barely audible whisper, said, ''He gives me the *creeps*.''

Amusement danced in his eyes. ''Why?''

''Because,'' she whispered intensely, ''he looks like
he'd like to grease his hands and run them all over me,
and I don't want anybody looking at me like that but
you!''

She clapped her hand over her mouth, astonished that
those words had come out of it. Looking up from under
her lashes, she expected to find laughter in Owen's
eyes. She expected some sort of sarcastic and suggestive reply. Instead, for a moment, there was the most
tender compassion she had ever seen on his face. Then
it was gone. He smiled slightly.

''Tell you what.'' He pulled his wallet from his hip
pocket and took some money from it. ''Take this.''

Her nervousness made her sound angry. ''What am
I supposed to do with that? Go to the movies? If you
want to talk privately, I'll just go home.''

''I don't care if you hear anything we talk about,

Sara. It's late and I'm hungry, and if I know anything, you are, too. Go have some lunch, on me.''

"I don't want to eat!''

He deliberately widened his eyes. "Like the Pope don't want to be Catholic! Bring us back a couple of steak sandwiches with fries and coleslaw.'' He took her hand and curled it closed around the crumpled bills. "I thought,'' he said more gently, "you could use a break from him.''

The warm touch of his hand was soothing. The gentleness in his voice eased her tension. She looked up and was able to say more calmly, "You know, Owen, in spite of what you—and some misinformed persons— say, you are the dearest man.'' Although she knew it was forbidden, she went up on tiptoe and brushed a quick kiss on his jaw. Then she gathered up her things and went out, skimming past Maddox with a confused word of apology.

It was still sprinkling rain, and she wasn't dressed for the short cut, so she drove down to Aunt Ada's. Robert's pickup was parked out front. She found him in a booth with Fiona Fitzgerald, a staid-looking brunette who had been a couple of years ahead of Sara in high school. After Sara accepted their invitation to join them, settled into the booth next to Robert, and exchanged long-time-no-sees with Fiona, she realized the young woman had been crying. A questioning look at Robert made him say, "I had to put Fiona's stud horse down, this morning.''

She should have known it would be nothing romantic. She was beginning to wonder if Robert had a romantic bone in his body. He was almost as bad as Haddon.

"I'm sorry, Fee. Robert always says it's the hardest thing to do.''

Fiona nodded and picked at her green salad. "I'd always rather do it than see one of my horses suffer, though. It's part of the business.'' She sighed and gave Sara a faint smile. ''Tell me what you've been up to.''

Robert's fettuccine primavera looked rich and full of vegetables, so she ordered it. She told her tale, omitting Kevin, making much out of her business classes and job, and minimizing her father's misery as much as possible. In the middle of venting her opinion of the revoltingly hot Phoenix summers, they heard sirens and craned their necks to see out the front windows. A police car whizzed by, followed by a fire truck and, moments later, an ambulance.

''Probably an accident up the Beeline,'' Robert said gloomily. When a green forest ranger's truck went charging by on the tail of the ambulance, he added, ''Somebody ran into a tree.'' It was too likely a possibility to be funny. As Sara settled back into the booth, she thought about the day the crazy driver had nearly run her down, about Owen's wishing the driver's close acquaintance with a tree, about hiding in his arms for those few lovely moments. Fiona had to do some prodding before Sara snapped out of her fantasy and finished her tale.

By the time she edited out the painful and personal parts, the last four years of her life sounded tedious. She steered the conversation back to the horse business by talking about Doubtful Ranch. Fiona eventually perked up enough to finish her salad and let Robert order her some pecan pie. Sara ordered the steak sandwiches to go at the same time. Ten seconds later, she felt the thud of a body dropping into the booth behind her and heard a male voice say, ''Never saw anything burn like that!''

''It's an old building,'' the man's companion responded. ''Tinder dry clear through, I reckon. It's a good thing there's been so much rain, or the whole forest might have gone up. All I can say is, I hope the Devil's got insurance.''

Robert choked on his coffee, and they twisted around in the booth together.

Sara saw vaguely familiar faces, faces that ten years earlier had probably been bearded, backed by long hair, and hooked above motorcycles, but were now shaved and reasonably respectable-looking. Old friends of Owen's, no doubt.

Robert said, "Hey, Calloway, did I hear something about a fire?"

The man with his back to them glanced over his shoulder. "Hey, vet. What's the idea of sending me a bill for putting my kids' cat to sleep? Good night, that broke their hearts! My littlest still cries herself to sleep every night because the cat isn't sleeping on her tummy. It's kind of adding insult to injury, sending a bill for something like that, isn't it?"

"Euthanasia takes my time and supplies," Robert said, "and I don't exactly enjoy it. What were you talking about when you sat down?"

The man on the opposite side of the booth said, "There's a fire up at Dixon's. We passed it on the way down. Pretty weird—you can't see the shop from the highway, you know, but we could see flames and sparks shooting up into the air above the pines, like some kind of big blow torch. I was saying—"

Sara felt as if two big hands had grabbed her lungs and were squeezing tightly. "Let me out," she gasped, shoving at Robert. "Let me *out!*"

He practically fell out onto the floor, saying "Take it easy, Sara. I'll drive you up, as soon as I pay—"

Sara left him talking to space. She was out and into her car and up the highway in seconds, all in what seemed like terrible, leaden slow motion. She had never thought of the shop as a fire trap, but now she realized that the front door was its only outside door, and it was at the end of that screwy tunnel—what had Owen's grandfather been thinking of when he built it, anyway? There was a fire extinguisher on the wall near the Duke Hat, a charming brass one that had probably been on the Ark. Did it even work? The Dixon men's idea of landscaping had always been to keep weeds away from the shop's foundation and out of the parking area and drive—it didn't run to flowers. Sara couldn't even picture the location of an outdoor spigot, let alone a hose.

A cop in a slicker stood where the shop's driveway met the highway, with his squad car and its flashing lights at his back, making sure no one got beyond that point. When she stopped and pointed urgently, he blew a whistle at her and motioned her off with his flashlight.

She might have argued her way past the policeman, but it would have wasted time and she wasn't sure how much of that she had. With a growl of outrage and frustration, she swung her small car around in a tight U-turn, and headed back the way she had come.

She ought to be encouraged, she thought in fragments. The fact that the police were there meant things were under control. And she knew that all sorts of other emergency personnel were on the scene, so everything would be taken care of. If anyone was hurt, someone would be there. . . . She forced the thought of someone's being hurt out of her mind and peered through the spotted windshield.

Owen's Aunt Ada short cut was well screened from the road by scrub. Sara spotted it only because she knew it was there. The car skidded off onto the shoulder. She fussed with things like turning off windshield wipers and headlights and locking doors, when those things shouldn't matter. She abandoned her fussing and tumbled out into the rain, hurtling up the trail.

Her shoes were designed for walking sedately on a dry, even surface. She slipped going up the slight incline in the wet pine needles, and somewhere near the shop's clearing, she promised herself Owen Dixon would buy her a new pair of stockings, because if he hadn't sent her on a sandwich run, she wouldn't be making this dash through the forest now. She could take the price of a pair of pantyhose out of the change she hadn't given him yet. . . . Well, she couldn't give him change when she hadn't made the purchase; the sandwiches probably were sitting back at Aunt Ada's, getting cold and soggy. She swore under her breath as she emerged from the sheltering trees into the drive. If Owen had taken Maddox to lunch instead of . . . He had only been trying to be kind, in his way, knowing how uncomfortable the other man made her. A break, that was what he had called it. He *was* the dearest man, in disguise. . . .

Fear was already choking her as she picked her way up the drive in her once-neat navy heels. More smoke lay here, eddying in the open space created by the driveway, which made breathing more uncomfortable, stung her eyes, and forced her to realize how much worse than what she had already imagined things might be. Behind her, she heard somebody yell, "Hey, lady! You can't go up there!" but it was from a distance, probably from the cop at the highway. She ignored him and kept going, and she heard no sound of following feet.

She realized why when she neared the top of the drive, where it widened into the parking area. Whoever had yelled had known someone would surely stop her here. The small graveled lot was crammed with people and vehicles, smoke and flashing red, blue, and yellow lights. They were restricted to the edges of the clearing—establishing a perimeter, she thought firefighters called it—back from the shop . . . the shop. . . .

The shop was virtually gone. Two blackened sides still stood, persistently licked at by flames. The front door, the tunnel, the incorrect hand-painted sign—only memories, now. Slightly to one side, Owen's pickup sat smoldering and doused by water from a fire hose. The front of the building still burned, sending up pockets of flame that the firefighters attacked with a stream of water. The roof had already fallen in over the office—where her typewriter and all of Owen's supplies and records were. . . . The neat presentation package for Maddox—all gone. All her cleaning for nothing. Owen. . . . Her throat closed up tighter. Her eyes stung nastily, and it had nothing to do with the smoke.

She hadn't expected so many people to be milling around, but slickers and uniforms were everywhere. There did not seem to be a fireman or policeman under seven feet tall on Payson's forces. Their radios chattered, uttering various beeps and whistles and bursts of static, along with their voices shouting back and forth to one another. Hoses laced across the gravel, some trained on the building, others directed at the surrounding forest. If the trees were to catch fire, there were homes up behind the shop that would be in serious jeopardy.

She started pushing her way around the outside of the clearing. Owen, if she knew him at all, would be as close as they would let him be to the action.

He would be devastated—wouldn't he? The way he had acted about selling the place, and the way his hard memories and feelings about his grandfather seemed so intricately tangled with it, she wasn't sure he would mind losing it. He would mind losing the business end, though, the orders, the tools, some of which were actually unique collectibles. He loved the shop and, at the same time, hated it, so would he be pleased or defeated by or indifferent to this? She'd know in a minute, as soon as she saw his tall, lean form with its cockily angled gray hat. . . .

She didn't panic for the few minutes it took her to make what seemed like a thorough search of the crowd.

She didn't really panic even when a big male hand latched onto her arm and a voice said, "Ma'am, I'm sorry. You'll have to go back down to the highway." She merely jerked her arm free, saying "I *work* here! I'm trying to find Owen!" and slithered away between a couple of slickers. That was an unfortunate choice of route. The slickers contained more cops, and one of them clamped a hand on her, while the one she'd gotten away from said, "Miss, you can't be here!"

"I won't get in anybody's way," Sara insisted, almost wriggling free. "I have to find Owen Dixon! Do you know where he is?"

Their answer was a silence that suddenly seemed ominous to her, and she looked up at the nearest face, half expecting to see a look of sympathy or regret.

Instead, the young policeman was scanning the crowd, maybe, she hoped, looking for Owen, too, or maybe looking for somebody to haul her away.

"I'm not leaving," she said stubbornly, then, "Don't I—are you Donna Foley's brother?"

He smiled faintly. "Yes, I am. You're her friend, Sara Dugan, aren't you? She told me about seeing you recently, and I know you worked for Owen, but . . ."

His use of the past tense was what did it. The buzzing that began in her ears must have come from the fire engine, or the redheaded cop's radio, or . . . She made a real effort to keep her knees from folding and demanded, *"Where is Owen?"*

"Look," he began reasonably, but yet another pair of male hands settled on her shoulders and turned her around, and she came nose to nose with a red silk tie.

Maddox's black suit and white shirt were no longer elegant, and his face was gray with soot. Worse, his expression was grim.

"You," he said, sounding as officious as anyone she had run into so far, "should not be here."

"I have as much right to be here as you do! More! Where is Owen?"

He hesitated. "I don't know."

"What do you mean you don't know?" She tried to shrug his hands off. "You were with him!"

"Yes, I was," he admitted. "He shoved me outside, then put his keys in my hand and told me to move my car and his truck away from the building. I thought he was right behind me!" He added gently, "I haven't seen him since."

A fist tightened in her stomach. Owen had to be there somewhere. People like Devil Dixon died doing something insanely funny or heroic, they did not die in fires. There was nothing in the shop so valuable that he would risk his life to save it. Was there? He didn't have a death wish. Did he?

"What happened?" she asked Maddox weakly. "How did it start?"

"There must have been an electrical short of some kind. We had gone outside to look at the roof, and we saw the lights go off. Owen thought a fuse had blown and was grumbling because he didn't have a spare. When we went back inside, the workbench was already burning. Owen yelled, 'Get out now!' and grabbed the phone to call the fire department. I tried to use the fire extinguisher, but I—couldn't seem to figure out how it worked." He looked sheepish. "Owen got off the phone and started cussing the extinguisher, then dumped half a dozen hats and the cash from the register in my arms, and pushed me out that peculiar hallway, saying he'd be right behind me. He added his keys at the last minute. It was quite smoky by then. I don't know if I'd have found the door without him pushing me toward it. He *was* right behind me! I felt his hand on my—"

They both jumped as a sharp crack from inside the burning shop, followed by another. The nearest cop demanded, "What *now?*" and they were all moving, ducking, looking for a better vantage point, fumbling under slickers for weapons and radios, wondering if some maniac were sniping at them from the trees.

Maddox pulled Sara back behind a squad car, from where she stared past the strobing lights at the shop, waiting for it to utter more epithets. Eventually light dawned. She called to Donna's brother, "Owen keeps a pistol under the counter. Could that be the bullets?"

The redheaded officer's eyebrows went up and he turned to a fellow officer for a private consultation.

Then a firefighter in a forward position yelled and dragged his hose back. Gleaming slickers scurried in the smoky rain. A moment later there was a straining sound, like a giant, spent log falling through the grate, as the rest of the roof gave way and plunged into the shop. Sara distinctly heard glass breaking—the mirrors, maybe, or the Duke Hat case. The antiques, she thought despairingly as she watched the firefighters surge forward again with their hoses, the lovingly made hats, the worn, rare, wide-plank floor . . . Owen!

In the wake of the new water bath poured on the fallen roof, smoke gushed into the clearing, wafted on a death breath of a breeze. Behind its curtain, someone was moaning. Someone was sobbing. Tears were adding to the indignities Bentin Maddox's neat silk tie had already suffered. Sara realized it was she who was moaning, and she who was crying, but she couldn't stop. She realized the arms around her belonged to a man she detested, but she couldn't seem to move. If no one knew where Owen was, if the cops didn't know, and the firemen didn't know, if Maddox hadn't seen him since Owen had shoved him down the tunnel, then Owen must have stayed inside, trying to save things, maybe even her stupid, highly replaceable typewriter!

A familiar voice insisted on knowing what was happening, and Robert's big, gentle hands settled on her shoulders. He sounded breathless as he demanded, "Sara, what's going on?"

Maddox must have told him, but Sara could hear only the roar of the blood in her ears—or maybe it was the sound of the still-burning logs of the walls of the Dixon Hat Company—Owen's coffin.

TEN

Owen dead. It was all she could hear in her head for a few moments. At least she had kissed him before she had left him last, but it had been a pitiful little Sara kiss on the jaw, enough to let him know she still loved him, but not enough to say how much. Not enough to say good-bye.

Robert was trying to remove Maddox's arms from around her, but she had the peculiar feeling that Maddox needed somebody to hold on to, too, at the moment. Maybe it had occurred to him that it could have been himself in the shop when the roof fell in.

"Sara," Robert was saying, "turn around." Pulling at her. "Sara!" An irritated-brother note in his voice. "Turn around. Let go of her, would you, so she can turn around, for gosh sake?"

When Maddox's surprisingly comforting arms released her, she made a truly heroic effort. She lifted her head and said, "I'm sor-sorry about yo-your tie, Mr. Maddox."

"Don't give it a thought," Maddox said gruffly.

She turned toward Robert, mopping her eyes with

her fists. "How—how did you—get in here? They didn't want to let me in."

"I told them I was a doctor." He grinned. "Look, babe."

She followed the direction of his nod, trying to see through burning, tearing eyes and thinking his grin was unfeeling but normal for a brother who didn't know how she felt about Owen.

A tall man came toward her out of the smoky rain, batting aside the hands of someone who was trying to stop him. He was filthy with layered rain and soot, and the left sleeve of his Western shirt was missing entirely, leaving a muscular, bloody, bare arm exposed.

Sara couldn't really see his face, but she knew his walk and his lean form.

She thought she was seeing things. *"Owen!"*

He held his good arm out and she was wrapped in it in a second, her arms around his neck and her face pressed against him.

"I thought you were dead!" she moaned against his neck. "The roof fell in and no one knew where you were and I thought you were *dead!* Owen, I thought you were *dead!*"

"Sh-sh-sh, I'm all right, precious."

His voice rasped. He was wheezing, trembling all over, but he was alive. She hung on to him as if he might turn into a wisp of smoke. She remembered that too brief and inadequate kiss she had given him earlier and lifted her hands to cup his face and bring it down to hers.

"Aw, Sara, don't, I'm all smoke and sweat—" He tried to continue, but she pressed her mouth to his and kissed him with every ounce of strength she had left. He was right, she discovered, but she did not really mind.

It was a short kiss. Owen abruptly jerked aside, staggered back, and began to cough. The man he had brushed away earlier appeared, the medical insignia on his jacket announcing he was a paramedic.

"Ma'am," he said, taking hold of Owen's arm, "you could help him if you'd talk him into letting me put some oxygen into him and look after his arm."

The bloody arm had scarcely registered before. It did now, and Sara looked at it in horror. "Owen, your arm!"

"Don't fuss" was his testy reply before he went off into another fit of gasping and coughing that went on until he was too weak to resist the paramedic's tugging and her worried pushing and nagging.

"You're buying me another pair of stockings," Sara said once he sat in the ambulance with an oxygen mask on his face, his gashed arm being dressed. He hadn't wanted her to hold his hand with Robert looking on, not to protect his own hide but to avoid confrontation with her brother for her sake. She held it anyway, in both of hers, tightly.

He looked at her skinned knees and shredded hose. "Happened?" he asked through the mask.

"I slipped on the needles coming up the short cut from Aunt Ada's." She held out her feet and twirled the toes of her formerly good navy heels. "I'm not exactly dressed for cross-country running."

She saw a weak grin flicker behind the mask. "Hey, little Sara. Where's my steak sandwich?"

Every girl Owen had ever dated in his misbegotten youth had become a nurse and worked in the emergency room. They poked and prodded him and wisecracked at his expense while he lay on a gurney, waiting for a doctor to stitch up his arm, keeping his mouth shut, for once, because his throat felt like pouncing paper.

A pristine white bandage decorated his left forearm when he finally walked out into the waiting room. One of his old girlfriends had been gentleman enough to clean up his face. He was aware of being aromatic and disreputable-looking, but compared to the alternative of being dead, it wasn't bad.

He had a couple of things to do that scared him. He didn't like admitting it, but truth was truth. He'd had enough adrenaline for one day, and he wished he could put off the chores that must be done, but he had learned, today, that things put off might never get done.

The waiting room was nearly empty, and Sara wasn't there. As he hunted her, he wondered if she had left. He wouldn't have blamed her if she had. It had been a long wait, and he'd made her stay away from him so he could think without the influence of her shy, wide, mother-hen eyes. He hoped she wasn't holed up somewhere bawling. He wouldn't have blamed her for that, either. He half felt like bawling himself, when he thought about the near miss he'd had that day and when he let himself think about the things that were dead and gone forever now.

He wondered if she'd done what he had asked her to do. She'd gotten that mulish look on her face when he'd told her what he wanted. She had wanted to stay with him, not run errands. Tomorrow, she'd reminded him, was supposed to be her last day of work, but she could always quit *now*. He had given that threat the respect it deserved.

Where the heck was she? He went back to the admitting desk and learned he'd overlooked the obvious.

They were outside under the overhang. The rain had stopped, but the eaves still dripped heavily. They watched the twilight, huddled together, he thought wryly, like a bunch of wet horses who turned and pricked up their ears when he came out. The reason for their being outside was obvious. Drew had a cigarette in his hand.

"Those things'll kill you," he advised in his scorched, raspy voice.

"Like you'd care," Drew growled in reply, tossing the cigarette into a wet flower bed.

Sara came and slipped her cold hand into Owen's. "All right?"

"More or less," he murmured. His conscience stung as he looked at her. She looked like a street urchin, her wet hair plastered to her head, her face smudged, her blue suit rumpled, and her knees bruised. She had, he noted, shed the shredded hose. Sara had very nice legs. "Nice to see you still here," he said to outrage her, which it did, judging by the look in her eyes. "Thanks," he added more loudly as Haddon slung a jacket around his shoulders and helped him slide his good arm into the sleeve.

"Sara said your purty blanket coat burned up. Her words, not mine."

Owen sent an appreciative smile to Sara, then looked at Drew. Scary chore number one.

"Thanks for comin' in. I wasn't sure whether you and the family had lit out for Colorado yet."

"We're leaving early Sunday morning. How bad is that?" Drew jerked his chin toward Owen's bandaged arm.

"Twelve stitches. I requested a satin stitch, but the doctor had no artistic sense." No amusement showed on Drew's face. Drew had never found funny a single thing he'd ever said. He sensed a question coming from Sara and added, "I don't know how I did it—caught it on something, but I had other things to think about at the time, if you know what I mean."

"What happened, anyway?" asked Haddon.

"Short in the steam pot, I reckon. It happened while I was outside with—a customer." He slid a glance at Sara. The fact that he had considered selling the shop was still nobody's business. "The lights went out; we went in to find out why, and the fun began—so to speak. I was able to throw some records and the books through the back window. And Sara's typewriter.''

Sara gulped and turned away, hugging herself. He wondered for the first time why she wasn't wearing a coat, and couldn't remember whether she'd worn one when she left the shop for lunch.

"I reckon I might have saved myself the trouble; the fire department probably doused it all with water. Anyway . . .'' He paused, looking at his eldest brother for a long moment. Scary chore number one, he told himself again, and took a deep breath that stung in his chest. "There was a minute there when I couldn't see, hear, or smell anything but smoke and heat. I thought I was dead.''

Drew's face remained dispassionate, which was actually encouraging.

"My life didn't pass before my eyes or anything,'' Owen went on, "but I do remember thinking three things, real quick, one after the other. One, Sara'll spend the rest of her life thinking I'm some kind of pervert.''

Drew's eyebrows went up, Haddon looked real interested, and Sara turned back toward him with her mouth slightly open. He didn't elaborate.

"Two, I owe Haddon fifty bucks.''

Haddon said gruffly, "It'll keep.''

"And, three, Drew will always think I hated him.'' He contemplated the older face that gave him a glimpse of what he might look like a few years hence. "I don't.''

Drew stared at him a moment, then made a small sound that might have been amusement or derision. He fished a cigarette from inside his jacket and began hunting for matches.

"It's time for the truth now, don't you think?'' Owen asked, because he wasn't sure if Drew was shutting him off or what. "God knows I almost missed the chance to tell it."

Drew flipped his match into the twilight and took a deep drag. At least he had the courtesy to turn away and blow the fog of smoke out into the open before he said, "My profession's taught me there's truth—and then there's truth."

"Yeah, well, mine is just the plain old truth, and the truth is I don't blame you for, Grandma's death. You were right about her. She could have died any time. She could have died pushing a grocery cart or hanging clothes on the line. You just happened to be there. I've been hidin' behind that—among other things—for a long time."

Drew listened, smoking, still impassive.

"And, the truth is, I'm sick of bustin' my face open on your knuckles. I give you my word—which, contrary to what some people believe, is worth something—I won't goad you about the money again. The truth is—you probably won't like this part, but truth is truth—Haddon and I never touched our shares until after Granddad died. It sat there and compounded all those years."

Haddon opened his mouth and took a breath, and Owen stopped him with a gesture.

"Haddon made the down payment on his ranch with his. I mostly paid for my house with mine. I'm not gloating about this in any way, Drew, I hope you understand that. You thought we threw our shares away years ago, and we knew the idea made you mad—so we never told you the truth, just to see your blood pressure rise. I want you to know the truth about it. I apologize for goading you with that all these years. It won't happen again."

Slowly, Drew turned his head and looked at Haddon. After a moment, he said, "And I always thought you were an innocent bystander."

Haddon shrugged casually. "Never know, do you?"

Drew opened his mouth to go on with it, but Owen cut him off before he could start.

"There's one more thing, Drew." This was the hard part. The words seemed to stick in his throat, and it had nothing to do with his singed vocal cords. "I want to say—in spite of everything I may have said in the past, and in spite of the fact that I don't always like you—I do respect you. You've done well in your profession, and you couldn't have done that without being a responsible, dedicated cop. I admire that. You've got a lovely wife and three great kids, which is a heck of a lot more than I'll ever have, and I admire and respect you for that, too. . . . I've said my piece. That's all."

He felt drained, suddenly. Sara had crept back beside him, still hugging herself, and he put his hand on her shoulder, more to keep himself upright than anything else. Drew was watching him, and maybe his exhaustion showed. He imagined he saw a flash of sympathy on his brother's face before Drew said, "You'd better let us give you a lift home."

He wasn't surprised that there was no gush of response to his peace-making. He hadn't really expected one. Was Drew's face still capable of a smile, or had his work driven all the smiles out of him? He squeezed Sara's shoulder and said, "Sara's running me home. Thanks, anyway."

Drew tossed his cigarette out into the wet evening again and, after a silent moment, said reluctantly, "I think Marcy and the kids'd like to see you again before we go back."

"I'll call you. Maybe we can set something up for Saturday, if I live that long." Drew didn't think that was funny, either. Come to think of it, neither did he. Owen glanced at Haddon, who nodded agreement and turned a commanding look on Sara.

"Take him home," Haddon said, "before he falls over." He pressed Owen's shoulder. "Don't worry."

He and Drew turned and went out into the parking lot. Owen stood there watching until they were in Haddon's pickup. Then he felt Sara give a shiver beneath his hand and said gently, "You're freezin'. Don't you have a coat?"

She gave a listless little shrug. "I—I did—I don't know what happened to it. Maybe it's at Aunt Ada's. I left there rather abruptly."

Poor Sara. He could imagine what she must have thought when she had seen the smoke or heard the sirens and realized what was happening. He knew what he would have thought had their positions been reversed.

"You are takin' me home, aren't you?"

"No," she said huskily, "I was planning on making you walk." She moved out from under his hand. "Wait here. I'll get the car."

He felt too lousy to argue, just stood watching her go.

She wheeled back suddenly. "Owen—I am so proud of you!" she gasped, then hustled away.

He leaned against the wall while he watched her cross the damp pavement. He couldn't have answered her even if she'd stayed. His chest had tightened up too much. Smoke inhalation, that was all it was.

He had to fold his body up carefully to fit it into Sara's car. He did so without grumbling—never look a gift horse in the mouth. The only real nice thing about it was that there wasn't much more than a hand span between them once he was inside. He leaned his head back with an unconscious sigh of relief.

Sara pulled out onto the Beeline and headed north. "Do you have a prescription to fill?"

He pulled the white square of paper from his shirt pocket. "How'd you know?"

"You forget, I have some knowledge of hospitals and doctors."

She sounded faintly bitter, and he rolled his head toward her on the headrest. "Dadgum, little Sara, I forgot. You must have had your fill of hospitals with your daddy."

"That would not be an overstatement."

"You should have said so. You could have gone home hours ago."

"I would not have gone home hours ago," she said softly, and he shut his mouth and swallowed. He seemed to have turned into a regular baby. It was shock, he told himself, and weariness. Everything everybody said to him made him feel like bawling. He deliberately turned his attention to her driving. He had never seen her drive before, he realized, not firsthand. He might have if he'd been able to deal a little better with Mel Page and those various other weaknesses that had driven a wedge between him and Sara years ago. He watched her hands and expression of concentration as she negotiated the wet streets, and was grateful for being alive to do it.

Sara took the prescription into the pharmacy for him. While it was being filled, she went next door to the market and bought a small sack of groceries. Back at the pharmacy, she tossed in a package of pantyhose and paid for it using Owen's lunch money with a clear conscience.

When she got back to her car, Owen was asleep. He did not look particularly comfortable, but he never would in that car—there was too much of him and too little of it. Asleep, he looked young and terribly weary. His bandaged arm was cradled across his body, and Haddon's jacket had fallen back from that shoulder. She gently tucked it over him before she took him home.

Owen's house perched up behind the golf course, set far back from the road, a solid, low pile of unpretentious golden logs nestled in among assorted conifers, scrub, and boulders.

The slightly inclined driveway ran around behind the house, but she pulled up where the brick front walk met the black pavement. She turned off the headlights, wipers, and engine. Rain pattered atop the car.

Owen didn't move. His chest still rose and fell rhythmically. Now they were even, she thought. He had driven her home while she slept, and she had done the same for him now. She hated to disturb him, but it was illogical to think of letting him sleep *there*. She patted his thigh and said his name.

He opened his eyes and stared upward for a moment before blinking and saying hoarsely, "The ceiling in my bedroom is much lower than I remember."

She smiled. At least his sense of humor had survived. "Dope. I imagine you wish you were in your bed, though."

"Amen." He lifted his head, moved his arm, and winced.

"Is it starting to hurt?"

"Some."

"The local anaesthetic they sewed you up with is probably wearing off. Better take a pain pill when you get inside so you can rest."

He nodded, then sat staring at the house as if he'd never seen it before. "I feel like lead," he said after a silent minute. "Why don't you come in?"

The invitation surprised her so much that she didn't know what to say. "That wouldn't be a good idea."

Slowly, he turned his head. "Do you really think I'm puttin' the make on you now, in the shape I'm in?"

"No," she said honestly, "I don't. I think it would be better if you had a bath and something to eat and went to bed. This isn't exactly the best moment for entertaining."

"Who said I planned to be entertaining? I want you to come into my house, that's all."

"I never have."

She said it gently, but he stared hard at her in the dark for a moment. "I know. High time. Don't you think?"

"Owen—the things you said to Drew, those were great. It was the right thing to do. But, you can't correct everything in one day."

"I know that, too," he said stubbornly. "Sara, will you or will you not take pity on a poor, wounded man—who probably got wounded trying to rescue your danged typewriter—and come in and make him a sandwich while he takes a shower, 'cause honest to Pete, he'll probably fall asleep in the middle of the kitchen floor if he has to do it himself."

She smiled. "Will it make you feel more comfortable?"

"Yes," he said firmly. "Pull around back by the kitchen door. Great," he rasped under his breath, "I just remembered, your friend and mine, Bentin Maddox, still has my keys—for all the good giving them to him did. My truck looked like a marshmallow at an arsonists' convention. I noticed he managed to move his BMW."

"He told me the first policeman arrived as he was starting to move the cars, and the cop wouldn't let him move your truck because it was so close to the building."

"I loved that truck. It was just getting broken in."

"It was just getting broken *down*. Anyway, he doesn't have your keys," she told him cheerfully, following the glistening drive along the length of the house and around its corner, where the kitchen joined the garage and its door jutted out in a porch that reminded her curiously of the shop and its tunnel. "He gave them to me after the ambulance had hauled you off. I think

I was wrong about him. He was actually very kind to me."

She positioned the car so that Owen's door was near the back steps, and they got out into the sprinkling rain, Owen moving cautiously. He saw Sara come around with the brown grocery bag in her arms and asked about it.

"I got some things while the prescription was being filled and you were snoozing in the car. I didn't know how well stocked your kitchen might be, and you didn't have lunch. I thought maybe some soup would feel good to your throat."

Owen looked faintly surprised and pleased. "To tell the truth, I'm almost too tired to eat, but, yeah, soup sounds not bad. Thanks, little Sara." He gave her a sleepy grin as he unlocked the door, knowing how easy it was to compliment her and irritate her at the same time.

The kitchen was cozy but not cramped, and well equipped. Sara was surprised and slightly ashamed of being so. What had she expected, a wood range and a hand-hewn bench? There was no dining room, just a nook in one corner for a small pine table and two chairs. Everything was blue and almond. Track lighting on the ceiling threw comfortable light and shadows into all the right places.

"Nice," she said appreciatively.

"Thanks." Owen was already working his one-armed way out of Haddon's jacket. "Make yourself at home. There's a bathroom across the living room. Better dry your hair and wrap up in that blanket on the couch. I'll turn the heat on and get in the shower."

"What about your dressing?"

"I don't know. I'll just leave my arm outside the shower."

"Plastic wrap?"

"Clever girl."

He supplied the plastic wrap. Sara gently wrapped his arm and they used Scotch tape as a fastener.

"See why I brought you in with me?" he said smugly when they were finished.

"This doesn't mean you can stick it under the water."

"Yes, ma'am. Maybe when I've gotten myself a little more presentable, you'll share that soup with me?"

"Yes," she said heavily, "as soon as you put on your tux and dancing pumps, I may do that."

"Sara," he rasped, going out a door, "you're such a smarty-pants sometimes, I don't even know why I like you."

"It's a mystery to me," she agreed amiably, watching his retreating lean, straight back. She stood there in his kitchen, in a foreign land in which she felt amazingly at home, weary and daydreaming, until she heard the water run somewhere in the house and knew Owen was in the shower. Then she did make herself at home, rummaging for a pan, spoon, and can opener. She found large blue mugs and put them on the small table. While soup heated on the stove, she decided to find that bathroom.

The front room surprised her wonderfully, as the kitchen had done. She had imagined Owen would create another kind of environment for himself, more like Haddon's house, perhaps, old, rustic, something like the house he had grown up in with his grandfather, echoing the atmosphere of the shop. But she had to remind herself that the shop had reflected the tastes of Benjamin Dixon. The fact that Owen had changed virtually nothing since the old man's death did not mean it was what he chose to live in.

The living room was open and airy. A large glass sliding door looked out onto a log deck. A stone fireplace crouched in one corner. A big, soft, blue sofa, flanked by easy chairs in blue-and-red plaid, lolled on an expanse of Confederate-gray carpet. An entertainment system—surprisingly high-tech for a man who hated typewriters—was just beyond.

Sara crossed the room and drew the drapes over the sliding door to keep out the chill, then went down a side hall that led her to a bedroom behind the fireplace. It was small and unpretentious, with a single twin bed, bureau, and writing desk all in gold-red pine. Nothing fancy. The bathroom opened from it. She frisked her hair with a bright blue towel and left it loose to dry.

She purposely avoided Owen's bedroom on the off chance that he might be making one of those naked dashes for some forgotten item that everyone made once in a while. Back in the kitchen, she opened another door and found a utility room containing well-loaded pantry shelves, a washer and dryer, and the furnace and water heater. A door led from there to the garage—an empty garage, she thought sadly, until Owen could buy another vehicle.

The house was smaller than she had anticipated, and while it was comfortable and cleverly designed, it wasn't particularly luxurious. It was cleaner than she had expected a bachelor's home to be. She accused herself of sexism after that thought, and went back to stir the soup.

When she heard the water turn off, she cut slices of Cheddar cheese and arranged them on a plate around a bowl of applesauce. She ladled soup into the mugs and put them on the table to cool. In the soft glow of the indirect lighting, the small breakfast corner looked snug and inviting. Pleased with the effect, Sara strolled into the front room and stood waiting for Owen to come out.

After a couple of minutes, she began browsing through his old LP's. The presence of Willie Nelson and Jean Shepard didn't surprise her, but the Chopin collection and an album of Strauss waltzes did. There was a small CD cabinet, nearly empty. He was just getting started there.

A plaid stadium blanket, like the one that had been over old Benjamin's big, cozy chair, draped the back of the sofa. Sara smoothed it. She pushed her fist into a sofa cushion. Comfy.

Where was Owen?

She listened. Not a sound. When the furnace kicked in, she jumped at the sound, then headed for the door that lead to Owen's room.

Like the rest of the house, the master bedroom was comfortable but not luxurious. There was space enough for a king-size bed and a full bookcase and larger dresser and mirror. The bathroom was to the left, the door standing open so that light fell out in a ribbon across the bed. Owen lay on the bed, face down, his injured arm stretched out to one side, in a pair of Levi's and nothing else, sound asleep.

Sara quietly went into the warm, moist bathroom. Owen's damp towel was puddled on the counter and the wet bathmat lay on the floor. Now *this* was more like what she had envisioned. She hung up the wet articles. The prescription bottle sat on the counter. A pain pill would have knocked him out, not to mention his harrowing afternoon, his injury, and the hot shower.

She left the bathroom, pulling the door most of the way closed behind her but leaving the light on. She peeled back the quilt that served as a bedspread, carefully avoiding jostling Owen's arm as she tucked the quilt around him. He didn't stir a muscle, dead to the world. Gently, she touched his hair. It was damp. She hoped he wouldn't catch cold on top of everything else.

Conscious of playing mother hen again, she returned to the kitchen and poured the soup back into the pan on the stove. He needed the rest much more than he needed canned soup.

ELEVEN

In Sara's dream, the Dixon Hat Company was on fire, but somehow Bentin Maddox was the one trapped inside. His strange green eyes peered at her from a window where no window should be. She and Owen stood outside, watching the building burn. Owen said, "I got the keys to his car," and Sara added, "I got you his red tie!"

She blinked awake on Owen's sofa, feeling guilty about the dream and cramped from sleeping against the couch's arm. She could still smell the soup, and her stomach reminded her of the supper she had missed. She got up, straightening her clothes and hair. It was too dark to see her watch, so she padded, barefoot, into the kitchen to look at the oven clock.

Eleven. Robert would be beside himself. She picked up the phone and dialed, but got her brother's answering service. At least, if he were out on a call, he might be too busy to notice his baby sister wasn't home yet. He had a brother's way of forgetting conveniently that she had been her own responsible person for several years now. Saying where she was didn't quite seem prudent. Her message said she was fine and not to worry.

She ate a piece of cheese to quiet her stomach. Then, because she was wide awake and didn't know what else to do with herself, she crept into Owen's bedroom.

By the light from the open bathroom door, she could see he hadn't moved. Carefully, she sat on the edge of the bed and found his good arm beneath the quilt. She rubbed it gently and murmured his name. Finally he started to stir, but groaned into the pillow and froze.

"Careful of your arm," Sara said.

His muffled voice rasped, "I wish you'd said that sooner." Slowly, cautiously, he turned onto his back, asking sleepily, "Is supper ready?"

"I think you should look at the time."

He rolled his head toward the digital clock on the night table.

"Eleven-fifteen?"

"Time flies when you're having fun."

"Aw, Sara." He sighed, disengaging his good arm from the quilt, and hunted for her hand. "Sorry if I wrecked dinner."

"Canned soup, Owen. Impervious to practically everything. I should leave soon, before Robert sends out a search party. Shall I fix you something before I go, or would you rather go back to sleep?"

He didn't speak for a moment. Then, "You care, don't you?"

"That's a really stupid question."

"No, I mean—it matters to you whether I'm comfortable or not. Happy or not. It always has, hasn't it?"

She pulled her hand away from his. "I told you before—I love you. I've always loved you, so, of course, those things matter. I wish you could understand that."

"You may not feel that way when I've told you—something I need to tell you."

"There is nothing," she said calmly, "that would

make me stop loving you. Shall I put the soup on to reheat?''

"I'm not hungry. Sara—"

"I'd better go home, then. If you need wheels tomorrow, you're welcome to mine.''

She started to stand. His hand circled her wrist.

"Sara,'' he said, his voice rasping curiously in his throat. "don't leave.''

Her heart kicked her breastbone. "I don't think that would be a good idea. Robert—''

"Mother-henning runs in the family, does it?''

"Robert's fussy.''

"Phone Robert.''

"I did. He must be out on a call. I left a message with his service.''

"Telling him you were here?''

"Ha. You already escaped death once today.'' She freed her arm and stood, moving off from the bed.

Cautiously, Owen tossed back the quilt and, holding his injured arm at an awkward angle, followed her, his tall, lean, bare torso gleaming in the friendly bathroom light. "Sara, I just about died today—scared the daylights out of me. I saw what I hoped was going to be my life's work go up in flames in front of my eyes. My tools, some of them custom made and one of a kind, are gone. The shop—a major part of my life for so long—is gone. My truck's gone. I might have lost you if you'd been there. I nearly ripped off my arm. It aches. Everything else aches. I feel like a truck ran over me. I'm tired and old and—lonesome.'' His tone was gruff. He caught her hand and stroked it with one gentle thumb pad. "I've been lonesome a lot of times in my life, but I never admitted it before. I don't want to be lonesome tonight, Sara.''

The movement of his thumb drove small, warm bursts of energy up her arm. She gave a little moan. "This isn't fair!''

"What isn't fair?"

"You are the one who said we had to be friends, only friends! Now you're asking me to spend the night with you?"

"If a man can't ask his best friend to stay the night with him, who can he ask?"

So now she had been elevated to the status of *best* friend. She didn't know whether to smile or scream. "Gee. How many women could resist a line like that?"

"I don't know, I've never used it before. . . . Did it work?"

Maybe, if he hadn't already been so hurt and sore, she would have done something violent to him. Instead, her voice quivering with a sudden mixture of emotions, she replied, "Oh—yes, I guess it did."

"Good." He grinned and dropped her hand. "I'm going to, uh, make a pit stop, and . . ." He went around the bed to the dresser and rummaged in a drawer. "You can put this on."

He tossed a mass of soft cloth at her. She caught it. "This—what's this? What for?"

"Sweatshirt. You don't want to sleep in that suit, do you?"

The light fell on her face now that he had moved, and he could see the uncertainty in her big brown eyes. He smiled. "I'm trusting you not to ravish me in the middle of the night." She continued to look at him over the wadded sweatshirt that she held to her chest. Gently, he said, "Trust me, little Sara?"

Slowly, she nodded her assent.

"Good girl," he said softly, and went into the bathroom.

The second the door clicked shut, Sara scurried across the living room and into the other bathroom, and was out of her clothes and into a hot shower. She hadn't realized how chilly she had been all day until then. It felt so good she had to force herself out.

In the light, the sweatshirt turned out to be maroon with a big gold Arizona State University logo across the front. It was huge, reaching nearly to her knees. The sleeves didn't want to stay pushed up. She would ask Owen to lend her a pair of socks, and that should about cover her entire body. Her hair had gotten damp in the shower again. She left it loose and, uncertain of what was coming, went slowly out into the living room.

She could smell the soup again. When she poked her head into the kitchen, Owen was there, clumsily using one hand to reassemble what she had fixed earlier. He had put on a gray sweatshirt with the sleeves slashed off, something that would easily accommodate his bandaged arm.

He glanced up at her from the cheese, then away, then back again in a classic double take. He looked her over from head to toe, then snickered.

"You could hold a livestock liquidation sale in there, if you wanted."

She smiled. "Does this actually fit you?"

"No. It was a present from—never mind. From somebody I knew a long, long time ago, who had an exaggerated idea of my, uh, proportions."

He meant a woman, of course. "May I please borrow some socks?"

"Sure. Top drawer, center. Some of 'em don't even have more than two or three holes."

"Leave that for me to do," she advised as she headed for his bedroom. "You'll hurt your arm."

"What you mean, but're too kind to say, is I'll break something."

She found a pair of thick tube socks that came nearly to her knees. Not bad.

Owen looked pleased with himself when she came back to the kitchen. All he had really had to do was take the plastic wrap off the cheese-applesauce plate and put the soup pan on the stove. He allowed her to ladle the soup, then they sat across from each other in the nook, eating like elegant pigs.

Eventually, Owen said, "I like this."

"Vegetable beef has always been my favorite. It's medicinal. My mother gave it to me when I was little whenever I felt bad."

"I didn't mean the soup. You miss her sometimes?"

She shook her head. "I think I got over that long ago. I was lucky to know her before she died. So many children don't have that chance."

He was silent as he finished his share of the soup. Then he pushed the mug back, turned down an offer of cheese with a shake of his head, and said quietly, "I guess I was lucky that way, too. . . . There's something I want to get off my chest."

"A tattoo?" Sara asked mischievously.

Amusement flickered in his eyes, but he said, "I'm serious."

She wiped her mouth and put her napkin down. "So am I. I know what happened this afternoon makes you want to run around and make everything right with everyone as soon as possible in case you don't have another chance, but you're overreacting! You'll have plenty of chances, and you simply can't fix everything in one day."

"Maybe not." He tossed his napkin onto the table, too. "I don't see any point in postponing a thing I can make right now, though. There's something I need to tell you, and I want to do it before I lose my nerve."

She sighed. "You don't need to tell me anything."

"Don't tell me what I need! *I know what I*—" He broke off, coughing under the strain of raising his voice. He coughed until Sara fetched him a glass of water and he drank. Then he gasped, "*Shoot.*"

"I'm sorry."

"Great, I was yelling, and you're sorry. If you say

one more mother-hen type of thing, I'll—strangle
you."

She chuckled, patting his back and clucking like the
mother hen she was. "I meant I was sorry for presump-
tuously thinking I know what you need. I have no idea
what you need. Really. I don't—"

"Shut up!" It was whispered as he wrapped his good
arm around her and brought her down into his lap.

Startled, she let out a yelp and giggled as he buried
his face in her hair, his mouth breathing warm air
against her neck. He didn't kiss her, and she didn't
speak. The giggles died away, and she let her head rest
comfortably against his.

"You smell good," he murmured at last. "Soapy."

"Was I supposed to rinse that white stuff off?"

He chuckled, but faintly, to keep from starting another
coughing fit. He raised his head and looked at her from
a couple of inches away. "You ready to hear me out?"

Being so close, cradled gingerly against his bad arm,
her face near to his, she felt suddenly very warm and
shy. She nodded silently.

"I want to tell you about that Halloween five years
ago."

Her shyness vanished in irritation. "I don't want to
hear that! I told you before, it doesn't matter to me."

"It matters to me! What I did that night built a fence
between us that's been up for five years! We could chat
through it. We could take pot shots at each other through
it. We could wave at each other through it." He waggled his fingers at the refrigerator. "We couldn't do
better than that. I could have torn it down any time,
but I didn't do it because—I'm a coward. My ego
couldn't take it, more than anything else. When you
were in Phoenix, I can't say how many times it kept
me from picking up the phone and trying to call you,
or trying to find you when I was down there because

I thought you didn't want me to. I want that fence out of the way. Now.''

Sara knew where he was going now, and she found herself shaking. She wondered if he could feel it, or if it was all internal. His pupils were wide from the shadows of the corner, or perhaps from the pain medication he had taken. Silently, she looked into his darkened granite eyes, then she said, "Go."

He tightened his good arm across her, as if to prevent some anticipated escape. He began slowly, reluctantly, softly, with a little gulp of air. "That night—that Halloween—was the night Mel told me she was pregnant. And that night was the first and only time I told anybody—except Haddon—that, whoever the father of her baby was, it couldn't be me, because . . . I'm sterile.''

He could feel the little jerk her body gave in his arms. He closed his eyes, waiting for her reaction.

She wanted to smooth the creases of worry from his brow, but she just said, "What did she say?''

"She laughed," he said, almost whispering. "She probably didn't mean to be hurtful. I'd let her go on and on—I think I was too shocked to say anything—about how glad she was to be having this baby and all the wonderful plans she'd made for us as a family. . . . I couldn't take it anymore, and I opened my mouth and the words came out. She looked at me for a minute, then started laughing. . . . I think it was just because she realized she'd put her foot in it up to the hip and thought it was a pretty good joke on her.

"She had a hard time stopping, so I got up and went around, collecting things that belonged to me. She tried to stop me by telling me how much she loved me and that it was just something that had happened—it didn't mean anything to her." His mouth twisted in a bitter smile. "Maybe I could have understood if she'd said she'd fallen in love with the guy, but she didn't. It didn't mean anything. . . . I loved her, Sara. At least, I

thought I did. I thought she loved me. I trusted her—
further than I'd ever trusted anyone since I was a kid—
and I got a boot in my gut for my trouble.''

The bitterness oozed out of him in his sandy voice,
and tears nearly started in Sara's eyes. Carefully, she
slipped her arms around his neck. "I'm so sorry."

He shook his head as if to say that it didn't matter
anymore, or that he didn't want the sympathy, or he
didn't want to be interrupted. "I drove around awhile.
I was miserable—goofy, I guess. Finally, I decided I
wanted to see you. I don't know why—you were just
a kid, I wouldn't have told you about it—but you always made me feel good, and I needed to feel
good. . . . Your daddy told me where you'd gone. I
nearly choked when I saw everybody was in a costume.
I thought I'd go crazy figuring out which one was you.
Your dad-blamed green frog was all padded up. I'd
seen you a couple of times before I finally figured out
it was not some squatty, fat girl, but my elegant little
Sara."

She wriggled slightly at the compliment, looking at
him from beneath her lashes and smiling a little. He
returned the smile, but it faded as he said, "I went a
little crazy, I guess. I don't think I was aware of wanting you that way before then. But—I want you to know
I wouldn't have hurt you. I wouldn't have—forced you
or pushed you any—"

"I know!" she whispered fiercely, tightening her
arms around him. "I know that!"

"When Haddon popped in," he went on doggedly,
"I had already realized you were scared and I was
hurting you, instead of—otherwise. I was already stopping—"

"I know. Owen, I know." She kissed him to make
him stop, and he turned his head to catch her mouth
hungrily with his. His hand slid up over her ribs and
tenderly cupped her breast through the giant sweatshirt,

almost as if he were showing her that it didn't have to be like it had been that first time, that it could be gentle and sweet, while his tongue delicately teased hers and his mouth loved hers.

He broke away first and cleared his throat, his breathing quick and light. "I went somewhere and got drunk that night. Woke up next morning in my truck—didn't even know where I was. Guess I didn't really know where I was all that next year." He shook his head, eyes closed. "I've been a coward."

"No, you haven't!"

"*Yes.*" His breath shook. "Sara."

"Owen." She put another small kiss on his shadowed jaw, his whiskers scrubbing her lips and making her shiver in his arms. "It's all right. It's *all* all right, Owen."

Motionless, he let her kiss him again. He let her lips brush down along his neck, and he let her head rest comfortably on his shoulder for a moment. Then he moved, dropping his hand away from her breast and letting it lie heavily on her thigh.

"Sara."

"What?"

"I just told you I'm sterile. I can't have kids."

"I know."

"Call me paranoid," he said with a note of sarcasm, "but I consider that something of a bombshell. All you did was give a little jump, but you didn't say anything. I don't suppose you'd want to tell me why."

She had been dreading this moment for years. She sighed. "Not particularly."

"*You knew!*" He wrapped a hand around one of her shoulders and jerked her upright so that he could look into her face. "Doggone it, don't play that hide-behind-the-lashes game with me now! You knew! How—" He stopped, understanding dawning on his face. "Haddon.

He was the only one who knew. He gave me his word," he finished bitterly.

He let go of her shoulder abruptly. She had the feeling that if she had been some small item, he would have flung her away.

"Owen, he *hated* breaking his promise to you, but he was positive you wouldn't tell me! He didn't want me to go around for the rest of my life thinking you were some kind of pervert—your words, remember, not mine," she reminded as he looked at her sharply. "I ran in to him two days after Halloween, and I was so embarrassed—I couldn't even look at him, let alone talk to him. He took me off in a corner and told me—and I'm willing to bet you have never seen his face redder than when he had to explain to an ignorant eighteen-year-old girl he didn't know very well what can happen when a seventeen-year-old boy gets the mumps! He made me give my word I would never tell a soul. I haven't."

He stood up abruptly, strong thighs that could aid a man in flanking a fat calf lifting them both, allowing her to take a controlled slide until her feet hit the floor.

"Owen, please don't be mad at Haddon. He was trying to help us."

Carefully, as if afraid he would break her, he steadied her with his good hand. Then he turned and walked out of the kitchen without a word.

Sara sat down abruptly on the chair he had vacated, shocked and muddled. She watched the door, certain he would rage around for a few moments, then come back—that was his way.

He didn't. Not so much as a creaking floorboard gave her any clue as to where he had gone.

She felt like a dinghy towed out to sea and cut loose to drift. What could she do? What could she say? She hadn't meant to hurt him, he already knew that. If she had wanted to hurt him, she would have told him of her knowledge and laughed in his face, as Mel had done, or she would have told everyone she knew that local stud, Devil Dixon, was only half a man. She had done her best to keep everything the way he wanted: silent. She and Haddon had never snickered behind his back about his inability to father children. He had said he wanted the fence down, and it was all down now, wasn't it? What did he wish she had done instead? Told him immediately? Plugged her ears when Haddon had told her? Lied by pretending she hadn't known?

Gnawing her lip to keep back tears of confusion and hurt, she slowly began cleaning up the remains of their meal, ears straining for any sound from Owen. There was none. The fence had become an iron curtain.

When she finished in the kitchen, she returned to the small bathroom and changed back into the navy suit and her battered navy heels. Her weary feet dragged through the living room. She left the sweatshirt and socks on top of the washing machine in the utility room, then reached to switch off the track lighting before going out the back door.

Movement in the doorway from the living room froze her at the switch, her hand in midair.

Owen stood in the doorway, his face in shadow. He asked hoarsely, "Leaving?"

"I thought you'd want me to."

Slowly, he shook his head. Uncertainty showed in his gray eyes. "It's just—It's so—I can't—" He grinned derisively at his own inability to go on. "It's like I said, a man will never understand how it feels to give birth. I—I don't know how to explain to a woman how it feels for a man to know he can't make a child. . . . He doesn't feel—*whole*."

She took one slow step toward him, twisting her purse strap in her hands. "Did your grandfather know?"

"Oh, yeah." His voice turned ironic. "I was still a minor then. The doctor told him first."

"He did this to you," she said with bitter certainty. "He made you feel this way."

"He never said a word, but I knew what he thought by the look in his eyes. I knew. He expected I'd start wearing nail polish and pantyhose any second." He shifted his bandaged arm as if sudden pain had shot through it. "I've told myself a million times I didn't have to prove anything to him or anybody, but I'm not sure I ever convinced myself."

"You don't have to prove anything to me."

He watched her silently for a moment. "You don't mind, do you?" He sounded faintly amazed. "I can't have children. You don't mind."

"No," Sara said softly. "It doesn't make you less strong, or less a man. Not to me."

"I thought you'd want children. I've never known a woman who, when you got past all the sex and other nonsense, didn't need her own child to feel . . . complete."

"Yes, you have. Me. The only time I've ever felt incomplete was when I was away from you. Anyway, there must be lots of children who don't have parents— who'd love to be adopted by a Mother Hen and a Devil."

"Are you sure, Sara? I mean it. You have to be *sure*."

"What do I have to *do*, Owen? Tattoo it on my nose? *I love you!*"

He held out his good arm and said, "Devil's through sulking now."

Her purse hit the floor as she went to him, throwing her arms around him and reaching her mouth to his. He lifted her with his good arm and put her on the counter, pressing her head back against the cupboard door, kissing her deeply and long, as he had never kissed her before. There was love in this kiss, sweet and hot, a first-time acknowledgment so sweet that Sara's damned-up tears flowed over, down her cheeks, into his mouth.

He released her mouth slowly, sipping her tears, following them up to her eyes, placing small, gentle kisses there.

"Don't cry, precious," he whispered. "Please don't."

"I'm—I'm not cr-crying!" Sara lied boldly, holding her face exquisitely still for the long-awaited kisses.

Owen gave a wicked, sardonic laugh and drew her closer, carefully wrapping his injured arm around her, too. "Liar . . ." He took another kiss. "I've corrupted you, precious girl. . . . Oh, we belong together, little Sara. We've always belonged together."

"You idiot," she gulped, "I've been trying to *tell* you that!"

EPILOGUE

The old-timers—those who'd lie in the Payson, Arizona, Pioneer Cemetery—got good conversational mileage out of how different the new Dixon Hat Company was from the old. There were no quirks in the architecture such as the old shop had had. Low and L-shaped, still in heavy logs but with that modern track lighting and big, triple-paned UV insulated windows, it sat away from the Beeline, as south as it could sit and still be in Payson, on a high piece of rocky land that had a view to kill for on a cold winter morning. No wonder Owen had decided on those big windows. Not that anybody really thought it had been his decision.

They said Owen had had the sense to keep full replacement coverage on his insurance, so once the new version of the shop had been built, a couple of slow, weekend trips in Owen's new pickup had provided enough credible antiques to refurnish. There'd been some hang-up about tools—it wasn't like you could just stroll into Sears and buy hatter's tools—and the wet winter didn't cooperate much with their building schedule, but it was a pretty small project, and they'd managed to open up by late spring. There were varying

219

opinions on what Benjamin Dixon would have thought about the computerized cash register and the CD player. Nobody could really carp much over the fire sprinklers.

Then there was the business about the Duke Hat. Some of Benjamin's old friends were delighted when an interview with Owen in the *Roundup* revealed that the hat had been saved from the fire by his having shoved it out the door in the arms of an anonymous customer. Delight turned into outrage when another article, a couple of months later, told how the hat and the autograph inside it had been authenticated in Los Angeles (everybody knew no good thing had ever come out of Los Angeles!) and had subsequently been sold to the Maddox Western Wear family to be part of a collection in a museum they were opening at their new Scottsdale headquarters later that year. They were also bidding on a likewise authenticated complimentary letter to Benjamin Dixon from George Phippen. Benjamin would either have jigged with relish or rolled over in his grave, depending on your view.

Then there was the matter of Sara. There were snide rumors at first. He'd got her in trouble and Robert had made him do the right thing. Sara'd lied and said she was pregnant when she wasn't, to trap him, like that other girl—what was her name?—had tried to do years back. They weren't really married, they were just living in sin and pretending so the church wouldn't have a conniption.

Trouble was, a lot of the old-timers had been at the wedding, which they weren't likely to forget, as it had been Christmas Eve and Sara had maybe been one of the five prettiest brides in memory. It had sort of shocked everybody that she'd worn a long red satin dress, but you had to admit that the little bouquet of evergreens and mistletoe she'd carried had been an eye-knocker, and the mistletoe in her hair had made her fair game for every man there, no matter how old—

not that anybody'd behaved like anything less than a
gentleman, no indeed. With Owen standing there like
a proud hawk the whole time? Not likely.

Then there was the little fact that all you had to do
was see them together to know they were witless about
each other. Owen had that hungry, possessive look in
his eyes, and Sara always looked as if she'd—in a real
sensible, practical way, mind you—jump off a cliff if
Owen told her to. No, the snide rumors didn't survive
long.

Drew Dixon started coming back to Payson from
time to time. That was kind of a shocker, too, since
everybody knew he hadn't spoken a civil word to his
brothers since Hector was a pup. You couldn't say
they'd all turned great friends and buddies, but things
were better, no question. He seemed to like Sara—but
who didn't?

Sara was a pretty decent little apprentice, Owen
would say with a grin. Time went by, and he still said
it, and eventually everybody figured out that she would
always be an "apprentice," no matter how good she
got. It took some getting used to, the idea that a woman
might have made your hat, but you knew Owen would
never let anything of less-than-perfect quality go on
your head, so you learned not to worry about it. You
better. Meek as she looked, Sara would take a shaky
breath and tell you to your face if she thought you were
a sexist pig, and Owen would just stand there and let
her. Figured.

Between times, Sara sat in the little office she'd made
Owen include in the shop for her—you didn't have to
know them long before you knew she could get Owen
to do anything, if she tried—making her computer keys
fly. Writers from all over the country sent her manu-
scripts to be typed and printed and mailed back, ready
to go to a publisher and get famous. Knowing Sara was
almost like knowing an actual writer.

Devil Dixon? Well, he sort of died along the way. There was no memorial service, unless some women got together somewhere and sniffled a bit. He hadn't been a hard drinker for years, everybody knew that, but after Sara, there were no more women and no more crazy stunts—unless you count the time he volunteered Sara for a dunking booth, but that was for charity. Well, there was that other time when he participated in that mud steer wrestling contest and broke three ribs, but that was for charity, too, and he was laughing the whole time.

No little Devil Dixons came along to Owen and Sara. If anybody got biblical on them and mentioned Genesis 8:17—there's always some poor fool who will—Sara would pop out her claws and point out that "God said that when there were only eight people left on the whole earth! Do you think He meant for us to keep having children until they have to be stacked like cordwood?" She did have a point, and who'd argue with a fierce little woman like Sara, when her crazy man was always there beside her?

SHARE THE FUN . . .
SHARE YOUR NEW-FOUND TREASURE!!

You don't want to let your new books out of your sight? That's okay. Your friends can get their own. Order below.

No.112 MAD HATTER by Georgia Helm
Sara returns home and is about to make a deal with the man called Devil!

No. 82 CALL BACK OUR YESTERDAYS by Phyllis Houseman
Michael comes to terms with his past with Laura by his side.

No. 83 ECHOES by Nancy Morse
Cathy comes home and finds love even better the second time around.

No. 84 FAIR WINDS by Helen Carras
Fate blows Eve into Vic's life and he finds he can't let her go.

No. 85 ONE SNOWY NIGHT by Ellen Moore
Randy catches Scarlett fever and he finds there's no cure.

No. 86 MAVERICK'S LADY by Linda Jenkins
Bentley considered herself worldly but she was not prepared for Reid.

No. 87 ALL THROUGH THE HOUSE by Janice Bartlett
Abigail is just doing her job but Nate blocks her every move.

No. 88 MORE THAN A MEMORY by Lois Faye Dyer
Cole and Melanie both still burn from the heat of that long ago summer.

Meteor Publishing Corporation
Dept. 1092, P. O. Box 41820, Philadelphia, PA 19101-9828

Please send the books I've indicated below. Check or money order (U.S. Dollars only)—no cash, stamps or C.O.D.s (PA residents, add 6% sales tax). I am enclosing $2.95 plus 75¢ handling fee for *each* book ordered.

Total Amount Enclosed: $_____.

____ No. 112   ____ No. 83   ____ No. 85   ____ No. 87

____ No. 82   ____ No. 84   ____ No. 86   ____ No. 88

Please Print:
Name _____
Address _____ Apt. No. _____
City/State _____ Zip _____

Allow four to six weeks for delivery. Quantities limited.